London's Adonis

Also by Jane Shoup

Wright and Wrong in the Valley
Hidden in the Valley
Will of the Valley
The Restoration
Zan, Birth of a Legend
The Key
A Choice of Captors
Ammey McKeaf, Book 1~ The Chronicles of Azulland
Heirs to the Throne, Book 2 ~ Chronicles of Azulland
Into Shadow, Book 3 ~ The Chronicles of Azulland
Charity Cases
Santa:2020 The Final Ride
The Time Tunnel of August Kaplan
An American Baroness, Book 1~ Sons of Barons
Nearly a Marquess, Book 2 ~ Sons of Barons
Christmas at Manoria, Book 4 ~ Sons of Barons
The Stewart Women, Book 5 ~ Sons of Barons
Manley Georgine
Ruaun3
The Uncounted
The Barretts of Crimson Hall

Copyright © 2021 by Jane Shoup
ISBN: 978-1-7351648-7-8

Prologue

April 6, 1820

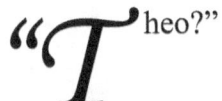"Theo?"

Had someone called her name? *Was she dreaming?*

"Theo?"

The voice seemed distant and unfamiliar. She'd been woken but by whom? Her head hurt terribly, and she felt too weak to move. She tried to open her eyes, but she couldn't.

Because something was over them.

That realization came with a sense of panic.

"Theo?"

She tried to answer, but little sound came out. She moaned and fumbled to reach up and touch her head. It felt odd. *Cloth!* It was bandaged.

"Theo," a different voice cried. It belonged to Cissy, her eldest sister. "She is waking!"

"Theo, darling," Laurel, her elder sister said. "We are here. Can you hear us?"

Her sisters hovered on her right side, each with a supportive hand on her. "My head," Theo murmured.

"Yes, love. You were badly hurt, and your head is bandaged."

Who was talking? Cissy or Laurel? How similar their voices were. This was not her bed or her room or their house. The feel was all wrong. The smell was wrong. "Where am I?" She could barely speak. Her mouth and throat were as dry as cotton.

"Theodora," an unfamiliar voice said. It was a deep, female voice. "We are going to sit you up so that you can drink. You need water."

Yes, she did. Desperately. She was lifted and supported. If not for being braced, she would have toppled; her balance was so skewed.

"Here we are," the woman said as a glass touched her lips.

Theo reached up to hold it, but only managed to bump against it clumsily.

"You are in hospital," the voice said soothingly. "I am Nurse Browning. I am here with your sisters, Narcissus and Laurel. The important thing is for you to remain as calm and still as possible."

Hospital? Dover did not have a hospital. "Where?"

"Darling, you're in London," Cissy replied. "You were brought here after the accident."

Accident? She touched the bandage over her eyes again. She wanted it off. Her fingers inched higher to find that much of her head was bandaged.

"The doctor will be here soon," the nurse said, removing Theo's hand from the bandage. She set it down and patted it.

Either Cissy or Laurel was crying. Or both of them. Why? What accident? They had been traveling to the city, she and Mamma and Greta and Rose. Why couldn't she remember more than that?

"Can you drink some more?" the nurse asked.

Theo took another drink. She heard footsteps approaching as they eased her back against fluffed pillows.

"Miss Martel," the approaching man said. "I am Doctor Josiah Holiday."

People shuffled about in the room, which was disorienting.

"I know you feel strange and weak," the doctor said. "You've been unconscious for days."

Unconscious. For days. Why? She remembered they'd been in the carriage, *no,* in a hired coach, going to the city. They'd gotten the bad news about Papa's condition, and they had been frantic to get to him. "Mamma," she uttered. "The girls."

"Let me ask a few questions," the doctor said. "And then we shall set about answering yours. Alright?"

She moaned from a searing shot of pain.

"We'll get you something for the pain very soon but, first, I need to assess your cognitive abilities."

Cognitive abilities. She'd hurt her head in an accident and they wondered if her mind was damaged. Was it? She felt horribly muddled.

"What is your name?" the doctor asked.

"Theodora Martel." Her voice was slurred. She licked her lips. "Theodora Elisabeth Anne Martel," she said, working to make the words clearer. Her mind was fine. She could not speak to how her head looked.

"Your age?"

"Twenty-three."

"What year is it?"

Her mind was fine. "Will you take the bandage off please?"

"Miss Martel, what year is it?"

"Eighteen twenty. Where is my mother?"

"Please stay with me, Miss Martel. Which of your siblings is closest to your age?"

She was frustrated by the questions. *One more.* She would answer one more and then she would insist on her own answers. "Laurel. She is twenty-six. My younger sister Greta is next closest to my age. She is nineteen. Would you like me to tell you their middle names and birth dates?"

"That won't be necessary. What is the last thing you remember?"

She sighed slowly, thinking about it. "Riding in the coach. Going to the city." Except she was in the city. She should have said 'coming here.' "My father—"

"Go on."

"He went … that is, he came here for tests. Medical tests. It's his heart."

She heard one of her sisters sniffle and then delicately blow her nose. They'd hoped for a miracle cure but had gotten a grim prognosis instead. *Papa.* He was so many things to so many people. He was their rock, and he would be gone in less than a

3

year. There was nothing to be done for it. They'd gotten the news but could not accept it.

"You recall nothing of the accident then?" the doctor asked.

She started to shake her head, but the movement hurt. "No."

"I see. The nurse will get you something for the pain now." He paused. "You should tell her," he added quietly.

Theo's breath caught at the dreadful phrase. It could only mean something bad. Something very bad.

"Is it not too soon?" Laurel fretted.

"It's best that she knows," the doctor replied. "It may help her remember."

Suddenly, Theo did not want to know. She jumped when she felt her sister's warm hand close around her arm.

"It was raining," Cissy uttered shakily.

They were going to tell her. And she did need to know. Whatever it was might be better than the horrible things she was imagining. She recalled the rain. A bitterly cold rain that fell so hard, they weren't certain the driver would be able to continue. She had rather hoped he wouldn't. She could tell Greta felt the same. The roof leaked. It was nothing short of miserable.

"The coach was not in the best of shape … we've been told," Cissy continued.

Yes. They had been told it wasn't, but Mamma had insisted on leaving once she'd gotten Papa's letter. "Where's Mamma?"

Cissy sobbed.

Why didn't they answer her? "Is she … dead?"

"Yes," Laurel replied, although she was crying, too. "I'm so sorry."

No. It wasn't possible. She'd asked the question to hear a denial. *Oh, dear God.* "The girls?" she choked out.

"Greta is fine,". Cissy said, struggling to get the words out. "Staying with me," she stammered. "You pulled her out."

Pulled her out? What were they talking about? Why weren't they saying anything about Rose? Did that mean she was gone too? *But, no!* She was only five.

"It's a miracle you're alive," Laurel said, enunciating clearly to be understood. "One of the back wheels of the coach went off the road and—"

"It went over," Cissy finished for her as best she could.

"Somehow, you got the door open … as it was going over," Laurel added. "You and Greta got out, but the others … there was nothing to be done. The coach was on the cliff."

The cliff. There was no surviving going over the cliff.

"Greta was able to scramble up, but you fell to a ledge."

Theo couldn't breathe. "Stop," she begged. God in heaven! No more words! No more explanation! They were lies. They were mistaken. She flailed and tried to get up, tearing at the bandage on her eyes. This was a nightmare. It had to be a nightmare!

"Theo, stop it. No!"

Hands tried to restrain her, but she fought them and ripped the bandage off. She gasped and stopped abruptly. She felt air on her face, and her eyes were open, but she could not see a thing. There was only blackness before her. She was braced from all sides, and her sisters wept uncontrollably. This was no nightmare. There had been a terrible accident.

Her mother was dead.

Rose was gone.

And she was blind.

Chapter One

August 7, 1821

*D*abney Adams, Dab to his friends, '*Adonis*' in the scandal sheets and gossip columns, accepted the squat crystal glass of whiskey from a silver tray offered by the maid who then promptly left the drawing room, leaving only the two men.

"Thank you for coming today," Sir Horace said to him.

"Of course." Dab sipped, and the whiskey was excellent, which was no surprise. The native of Yorkshire had made a fortune in textiles by the time he was thirty, and the success of his mills had never faltered. He'd begun life as a scrapper, willing to fight and claw his way to wealth. Now, he seemed a convivial man who frequently boasted about buying his baronetcy.

Dab was here for one reason, Cora Palmes, the man's only daughter and heiress to his fortune. It was a good reason.

"I thought we should talk man to man," Sir Horace said. "The papers have been full of innuendo about you and my daughter."

"Unfortunately, the papers are always full of innuendo," Dab returned dryly.

"Indeed. Especially where you are concerned."

Dab knew it too well.

"But she is fond of you," Sir Horace added.

"I'm fond of her," Dab returned evenly. After all, what wasn't to like? Cora was friendly and pretty. Her manners were excellent. Unlike her father, she had no Yorkshire accent to speak of. She was intelligent. Not terribly witty or clever, but they could carry on a conversation.

"Dabney ... may I call you Dabney?"

"Certainly."

"The thing is, Dabney, I do not want Cora encouraged if you do not harbor the right intentions."

Dab felt something clench inside, but he tried to remain expressionless. It was as if a bear trap had been placed in front of him. *Simply place your foot inside. It won't hurt much.* "Intentions," he repeated.

"For the future. For an attachment of the permanent variety." Sir Horace drew a pensive breath. "It's just that you have a reputation of being elusive to the point of ...I'm trying to think of the right word," Sir Horace mused. "Unattainable?"

Dab bit on the end of his tongue. He had known Cora Palmes for all of six weeks or so, and he was already supposed to have developed intentions toward her? Of the permanent variety?

"I sometimes take great risks in business," Sir Horace continued. "However, they are calculated carefully. How much can I gain? How much can I lose?"

Dab had no idea what one thing had to do with the other, but he nodded. He had assumed he was here to be evaluated, but pressed on his willingness to marry Cora? It was preposterous.

"But I am not willing to take risks with my daughter. She is too much of a prize, as we both know. Too much of a treasure to me."

It was definitely time to speak. "I understand," Dab said.

Sir Horace cocked his head. "You understand," he repeated as if vexed that was all Dab had to say. "It may offend you to know, but I've had you investigated."

It rather did offend him, but Dab refused to let it show. He took another drink. "Oh?"

"Yes, well, it was puzzling to me that you have lodging in Albany. I'll admit, it's an excellent place for bachelors, prestigious even, but usually it's the younger sons of nobility that live there."

"It suits my needs."

"You are estranged from your parents."

Dab remained silent for several seconds. "I do not see them a great deal."

7

"Although they are right here … in a fine home in Leicester Square. Perhaps not the prominent address it once was," he added smugly, "but still a good one."

"It is," Dab agreed levelly.

"It's not that I wish to pry," Sir Horace said.

Dab restrained a grunt. For someone who had no wish to pry, he did a superb impression of it.

"I am curious as to your plans for the future."

This conversation was precisely why Dab did not get serious with a lady. It was just not the lady; you had the entire family toc contend with. This interview, more like an interrogation, was making him feel suffocated. *None of your damn business,* is what he longed to say.

"Will you inherit the barony? I know there is no great fortune there. That does not concern me. I also know you have not been disowned, but this estrangement—"

Dab finished his drink. He wanted to put his glass down firmly and take his leave, but perhaps Sir Horace's inquiries were justified. "You're correct, Sir Horace. There is no fortune there. Not even close to it. But the barony is my birthright, such as it is Of course, I will accept it when that day comes."

"My word. You are closemouthed about yourself."

"I prefer to think of it as private."

Sir Horace smirked. "Really? London's Adonis. Private."

"I have never called myself that," Dab stated coolly. "Nor did I ever want to be called it. My preference is privacy, to never be written about at all."

Sir Horace rose and went for the decanter. He returned and refilled Dab's glass and then his own before sitting again. "Cora cares for you. That is the only reason I am asking."

"I realize that," Dab conceded. After all, he could appreciate a father's concern. Especially when it came to him.

"Forthright. Blunt. That is my way," Sir Horace declared. "It usually serves me well, but I can see that it may come across as … intrusive. Still, I feel an obligation, if you will, to better understand you." He paused. "Have you given any thought to where you will live in the future, say with a wife and family?"

"Honestly, sir, I have not."

The older man studied him. "I do not believe that you are in earnest pursuit of Cora's hand."

Dab could think of nothing to say. It was true, but was it wise? Cora was a fine lady with a fortune. If they wed, he would never have to concern himself with finances. They would never want for anything of a material nature. As for *love*, he wasn't the sort of man cut out for love. He had never been in love. Hell, he had never ventured close to the magical kingdom of Love. He knew it existed because he'd seen one friend after another venture inside its perimeters and then gleefully reside there.

"Well," the older man said. "My daughter has a mind of her own, but I will make my thoughts known to her. I fear she is under the mistaken impression that your feelings go deeper than they do."

The statement had been uttered with derision, a hint that he had no feelings, which made Dab prickle with resentment. "I have not misled her. Not for a moment."

Sir Horace pursed his lips and shrugged. "I imagine that's true."

"It *is* true."

"Thank you for coming today," Sir Horace said dismissively before he picked up a bell and rang it.

Dab set his drink aside, stood and bowed his head before leaving. It was possible he had just destroyed a chance to win Cora's hand and her fortune, so why did he feel a sense of liberation?

Chapter Two

*D*ab was about to leave to go meet his friends for dinner when he noticed a note that had been slipped under the door. He picked it up and read.

Dabney,
Your father is dying. Come at once. I will ask
nothing more of you. Please, son. I beg this of you.
-Mamma

He sighed and left. He walked a block before he got a cab. His father had been ailing for months. Stomach pain mostly, with on and off swelling. Had it grown more serious or was this just another and a far more desperate attempt to get him home? But even that, the desperation, was concerning if that was the case. Was his mother simply overreacting? She had never been the hysterical sort. Besides, he had a *feeling*. A sort of internal warning to heed the message without delay.

There seemed to be so much illness and death all the sudden. The queen had died only days ago of a stomach ailment. Now his father? What if he was dying? Dab rapped his knuckles against the seat thinking about it. Did he have it in him to forgive them? They had asked, but their pleas had always fallen on deaf ears.

When the cab stopped, he climbed out and paid the driver. He turned back to the house, mentally bracing himself, and then went to the front door. He knocked and the door was opened by the butler. Fanning stood there with a delighted smile on his face.

"You never need knock in your own home," Fanning chided with affection.

Dab stepped inside. "How are you, Fanning?"

"Very well, my lord. Better now. Oh, it's so good to see you."

"It's good to see you, as well."

"Dabney," his mother said from behind him.

Dab turned to the staircase as she came down with her usual grace. She looked as lovely as ever, but tired. Fanning left with a quiet tread.

She walked toward him but stopped a few feet away. "Thank you for coming," she uttered quietly.

"Of course," he murmured. "How could I not?"

"You should go," she said thickly gesturing up the stairs.

Dab stepped closer to her. "It's that serious then?"

Tears filled her eyes. She nodded. "He hasn't much time. All the doctors can do is help with the pain."

Dab blinked. Perhaps he should have been prepared but he wasn't. He was shocked and angry and frustrated and maybe a little bit frightened if he was honest. "Why didn't you tell me?"

A momentary look of anger crossed her face. She looked away and then back to him. "We told you he wasn't well."

"Not well and dying are two very different things, Mamma."

She lifted her chin. "Are we really going to stand here and argue? Now? You are here and he is still here. All he wants is your forgiveness."

Dab could think of nothing to say, so he stepped past her and started for the stairs.

"Dab," she called when he was midway up.

He turned back.

"You should prepare yourself," she said tenderly. "He looks … as ill as he is."

The door to his father's room was open. Dab's steps unwittingly slowed as he got closer. He reached it and peered inside to see his father in bed with his eyes closed, his face turned toward him. He looked yellow.

Let it be the light, Dab prayed.

His father opened his eyes and smiled. "Dabney," he said weakly. "I was just thinking of you."

Dab came closer. It was no trick of the light. His father's skin was horribly jaundiced. Even his eyes were yellow.

"I have looked better," Henry Adams said. "For that matter, I have felt better."

Dab couldn't speak for the lump in his throat. His father held out a hand toward him. Dab sat on the chair next to the bed and took hold of the cool hand. "I didn't know."

"You couldn't have. I took a turn and—"

Dab swallowed.

"Son, my affairs are in order. All but one thing."

Dab looked away and wiped at his eyes, loathing himself. He'd waited too long and now it was too late.

"We are so terribly sorry. We have been, you know. So sorry. We should have believed you. We should have believed in you."

Dab looked back at him and nodded. He should never have held his grudge so long.

"I'm sorry that," his father continued, "there won't be time for proper amends. Not from me."

Dab stroked his father's hand to warm it. He wanted to deny it. To say there would be time, but it wasn't true.

"I am asking for your forgiveness."

"Yes," Dab replied. He released a shaky breath and nodded. "Yes."

"Thank you." He winced and drew a sharp breath, as if in pain. "You cannot know how much it means to me."

"I'm sorry." He'd been a fool. He'd been a prideful fool and now there would be no making up for it.

"Dabney, your mother—"

Dab stiffened.

"Try. Please. She loves you so much. We made a mistake, but we have suffered for it."

Dab nodded. It was not exactly a promise, but he would try.

"Now, tell me about the season, *Adonis*," his father added with a wry grin.

Dab rolled his eyes and shook his head. "Ugh."

Henry chuckled. "How much of what we read is factual? I would wager not even half of it."

12

When Dab came downstairs an hour later, Fanning was waiting and looking proud of him. "Where is my mother?" Dab asked him affectionately. Fanning had been part of the household for his entire life.

"She's waiting for you in the drawing room, my lord."

"I'll see myself out. You needn't wait."

"Will we see you again soon, I hope?"

Dab nodded. "Tomorrow."

Fanning beamed.

Charlotte Adams stood with her arms tightly crossed as if hugging herself. "He laughed," she said through a tight throat. "I heard him. He laughed."

Dab nodded. "It was a nice visit."

"Thank you," she said.

It was so sincere that he sighed. "I should have come before. I'm sorry I didn't." He paused. "I'll return tomorrow, and I will stay."

She fought a surge of emotion, bowing her head, her hand pressed to the lower part of her face. She nodded but did not look at him.

He was unable to speak, so he turned and left.

Chapter Three

Most of the SOBs, sons of barons, Dab's closest friends, had met that evening for dinner at JG's home. JG was also Lord Blairwood, a marquess, and he would become duke when his grandfather passed. He'd be Morguston then. JG was not an original member of the SOBs, a group formed at Harrow when they were boys, but he'd been part of their circle for nearly a decade.

The right honourable Mr. Nigel Walston would be Lord Merton one day.

Hugh Pritchett's father was Lord Fitzwarren, but Hugh had two elder brothers, so it was unlikely the title would ever come to him.

Jonathan was already Lord Stewart, but Stewart was his surname. His adjustment had been in the acquisition of the barony, not the name. His twin brother, Joel, elder by a mere eight minutes, had inherited the title and then unexpectedly, inherited a marquisate from a distant relative. Joel had pulled strings to get the barony given to Jonathan.

Of their group, Joel would be the only one not in attendance this evening. He and his new wife, Jane, had returned to his newly inherited home outside Gloucester. Joel, who was now Lord Larrowford.

And himself? Soon, the barony would be his. He would be Lord Sonden.

Changing names. Changing stations. Changing lives. For the uninitiated, it was enough to make one's head spin. Dab was initiated, thoroughly initiated, and the thought of it was suddenly mind-numbing.

Lord Morguston's residence was nothing short of palatial. They did not usually meet there, but the old man had softened of late and given JG more freedom. Dab was two hours late as he was led toward the dining room. His friends were exiting it, so they all met in the corridor.

"There you are," JG said cheerfully.

"This is more than fashionably late," Jonathan scolded halfheartedly.

"Have you eaten?" JG asked.

"No, but I'm not hungry."

Hugh stepped closer with a concerned expression. "Has something happened?" The others quieted. They had been in a jovial mood until thirty seconds ago.

"I learned my father is dying. I was there."

"Dab," Nigel said. "I'm so sorry."

Hugh clasped his shoulder.

"So am I," Jonathan said soberly.

"You won't believe it," Dab said. "But, for once, I would have been early this evening. But then I saw the note from my mother. It had been slipped under the door."

JG looked at the butler. "Have cook prepare a plate, Ensley. We'll be in the salon."

Ensley, the butler, bowed his head and left.

"You have to eat," JG said solicitously to Dab. "You have to keep up your strength." He led the way to the salon. The sets of doors leading to the garden were open, allowing a welcome although humid breeze through as they took seats.

"So you just learned of it," Hugh said carefully.

Dab nodded. "I stayed away too long and now there will never be any making up for it." His friends remained quiet. They knew that his family was a touchy subject. One he'd made virtually off-limits.

"So you went there," Jonathan coaxed carefully, breaking the silence.

Dab nodded. "I saw my mother for a few moments and then went to my father." He shook his head. "He's yellow. His skin, his eyes."

"His liver, then," Hugh said softly.

"Yes. He really is dying. I know it. I saw it. I just can't quite … accept it."

"That's natural," JG offered.

"There is nothing natural about any of it," Dab retorted miserably. "That's the problem. There was nothing *natural* about any of it. That wasn't their fault, but then they didn't believe me. That was the mistake. And I have had them paying for it for sixteen years." He knew he wasn't making any sense to them, and he was overcome with emotion, so he looked away until he bested the urge to break down.

"We're here for you," Nigel said.

The others nodded. "Whatever you need," JG said.

They wouldn't press him for a clarification of his rant because they were the best of friends. "A drink would be good."

"Oh!" JG got up. "What am I thinking?" he added with a tap to his forehead. "Scotch? Whiskey? Sherry?"

"Yes, please. One of each with another right behind it."

That lightened the mood and they all chuckled.

"Scotch," Dab said.

"Coming up. Jonathan, what do you want?"

"Whiskey, but I'll help," he replied, getting up and following JG.

"Me, too," Nigel said.

"I'll have scotch," Hugh replied. He looked at Dab. "Do you want to talk about how the visit went with your father?"

"It went well." But what if he hadn't gone? He'd ignored their requests before. "I'm going back tomorrow and I'll stay."

Hugh nodded.

"Now, someone please talk of something else," Dab requested.

JG handed him a drink. "Hugh had news."

Dab looked at Hugh, who smiled. "I've accepted a teaching position at Cambridge."

"Congratulations," Dab exclaimed.

"Professor Pritchett," Jonathan said, lifting his glass.

"You already toasted me," Hugh laughed. "Stop already." He looked at Dab. "The contract is for the next term only, and it's on a trial basis."

"In history, I take it?" Dab asked.

Hugh nodded. "Late Middle Ages. 1250 to 1500."

"That's very specific," JG commented as he sat back down with his drink.

"Yes, well, there are lots of catastrophes to cover," Hugh said. "Famines, uprisings, the black plague."

Ensley entered with a tray.

"Thank you, Ensley," JG said.

"Yes, thank you," Dab said to the butler.

"Of course, my lord," Ensley replied.

The tray was set in front of Dab, the lid removed, and an elegant presentation and mouth-watering aroma hit at once, reminding Dab that he had not eaten in hours. Wine was poured for him, and his friends conversation went on. On the plate was sliced meat of some kind and vegetables in a light broth. Leeks, onions, mushrooms, carrots.

"So I won't be able to go to Manoria, as planned," Hugh said.

Manoria was Joel's new estate, and they had all planned to go in the coming weeks. It was unlikely Dab would be able to join either, but he couldn't think about it now.

"They are building another greenhouse," Jonathan said. "Jane is thrilled to bits. Even Lakely is excited about it. She claims she's going to help, but I can't see it, somehow."

Nigel grinned. "I can. I can picture them planting and chattering away, getting as dirty as they please. Lakely will bring out wine in the afternoon."

JG laughed. "I wouldn't mind being right there with them."

"This is delicious," Dab commented about the food. "What is it?"

"Do you want its proper French name or the translation?" JG asked.

"Either. Surprise me."

"*Blanquette de veaux,*" JG said with a flair.

17

It translated to a stew of calves. "Yes," Dab said. "The French version is more appealing."

Dab chose to walk home that night. The evening with his friends had been exactly what he needed, but now it was time to get his thoughts in order. It felt as if he'd been without direction for years, but things were changing. Destiny had reshuffled the deck and would soon deal its next hand, even if he wasn't ready for it.

Was the prudent thing to marry Cora and get on with life? Her father would buy them an elegant townhome and an elegant carriage, and they would have elegant children. Dab recalled the jest he'd made to Nigel about Alice when they'd first learned about her. *I wouldn't mind marrying an heiress.* Naturally, he'd been flippant at the time. They had all been trying to cajole Nigel who felt pressured into a match with an American he had not even met yet.

It turned out that Alice wasn't an heiress. She was lovely and passionate, and Nigel had fallen desperately in love with her. Cora was an entirely different matter. He did not love her. Was he capable of love? That question burned at his core. Was he capable of love or had he smothered the instinct years ago until there was no chance of reviving it?

Elusive. Unattainable. Inscrutable. The writers of newspaper columns and scandal sheets cited the descriptions as if they knew him. They did not. Did he even know himself?

He stopped and shoved his hands in his pockets as he looked up at a hazy half-moon. His father was dying, and there was nothing he could do to stop it or to make up for the years he'd wasted stymied by anger and resentment. He was adrift in an ocean of remorse for it, and he was achingly lonely.

Cora was not the answer. She would never eradicate his loneliness. Clouds covered the moon, and he sighed heavily as he walked on.

Chapter Four

Maeve had worried about Theodora for sixteen long months, although *worried* wasn't an apt enough word. Directly after the grisliest carriage accident Maeve had ever heard of, she had feared for Theo's life, and for good reason given the head injury the young woman had sustained, but Theo had survived it when her mother and youngest sister had not. She'd survived but regained consciousness to discover she was blind.

Horrible headaches had ensued, but they'd eventually faded, as had the blindness. At first, Theo was able to make out light, and then shapes, and then colour. All of it while dealing with the grief of loss and trying to comfort her ailing father who was devastated beyond redemption. Three months and two days after the accident, he too passed. They had known his condition was terminal before the accident, but his anguish over losing his wife and youngest child had sped the process.

With no one else on which to focus her care and attention, Theo's grief knew no bounds. On top of everything, they learned that her half-brother, Cyrus Martel, had sold the family home in Dover. The greedy pig. It had not been *his* family home. He was a product of his father's first marriage. His half-sisters were the result of the second marriage. It had been their family home, and it was sold without Theo ever knowing it was happening. Along with the furniture and the pictures and portraits and knickknacks and keepsakes.

Her personal possessions had been packed and shipped to the London townhome, where she was brought after the accident. Now Cyrus, Viscount Chausterforth since the death of their father, was selling the townhome for no other reason than to have more money in his coffers. The hateful, greedy pig! He had no compassion.

He had informed Theo that either she could move in with one of her elder sisters, knowing full well they did not have the room or financial ability to support her, or he would arrange a suitable marriage for her. He had two willing prospects in mind, Mr. Charles Pugh, a wealthy, part owner of a shipbuilding enterprise, or Sir Amos Pearce. Being the generous brother that he was, he would allow her to choose which of them it would be.

Maeve loathed him for it, pure and simple. Theo loathed him for it. Theo's sisters, Cissy, Laurel and Greta, all loathed him for it, but that was where Theo had been tonight, to a ball, her first in a year and a half, to meet the prospects that her half-brother had deemed worthy. Without doubt, Theo's marriage to one of them would benefit him somehow.

All her life, Theo had been the liveliest girl in the world, clever and so pretty with wavy hair a mix of gold and light brown, pale brown eyes, and a smattering of freckles across her pert nose. Now, however, she sat lifeless in front of her vanity in her oldest chemise. It was soft, nearly threadbare, the one she used for sleeping in the summer. Maeve stood behind her, brushing her hair and trying to get her to talk. Maeve had been the personal maid and friend to Theo's mother for thirty years. Scarlett. God rest her soul, there had never been a finer lady. "Tell me about it," Maeve urged.

"It was very grand," Theo replied drolly.

Maeve grunted. "I'm sure it was. I meant them."

Theo shrugged. "Not as horrible as I expected."

The reply had been uttered without a spark of feeling. "That doesn't tell me much."

"There isn't much to tell. I met Sir Amos first."

"And?" Maeve put down the brush and began braiding Theo's thick hair. It had been healthy and silky, but it was lackluster recently, like the girl's spirit.

Theo sighed. "I won't get any rest until I tell you, will I?"

"Probably not."

"Fine. Sir Amos is forty or so. He is a widower with no children. He was polite. Arrogant but not … insufferable. Cyrus informs me if I marry him, I will have my own income, plus I would be generously provided for. The man has a house somewhere in Mayfair. I can't remember the street. Not that I would know it, anyway."

"Well, I must say that description is dispassionate."

"We spoke, mostly he spoke, and I sipped lemonade. It's a bit early for passion, wouldn't you say?"

The words might have been construed as humorous except for Theo's lack of vitality. "And Mr. Pugh?"

"He is younger. Thirty perhaps. Never married. He's attractive. Successful, I'm told. But there is that name," she said with a frown of distaste. "Pugh," she said, drawing the name out.

Maeve chuckled as she finished the braid. Theo reached back to hold it as Maeve tied a thin ribbon around the base to secure it. "There," she said.

Theo rose. "Bed," she said tiredly, turning to Maeve.

"Theo, listen to me. Whatever your loathsome half-brother says, you don't have to marry anyone right now. You have your father's inheritance and that bit of money your mother left that Cyrus doesn't know about."

Theo sighed. "You know that won't last. Not even a year."

"In the meantime, we will figure out something," Maeve declared. "We can always go back and live in Spinster House. The spinster part won't rub off, you know. My siblings and I have made that choice for ourselves."

Theo smiled. "You are a dear. Now, go to bed. I've kept you up far too late." She kissed Maeve's cheek.

Maeve started for the door. "We'll discuss it tomorrow."

"I don't have long."

Maeve turned back. "What do you mean by that?"

"There is a ball in two weeks, an end of the season bash when engagements are announced as part of the entertainment."

Two weeks!

"Hib wants it done then."

Hib stood for half-brother. Theo had made it up years ago and she usually said it with a look to suggest she'd tasted a mouthful of green gooseberries. "He wants what done then? A decision?"

Theo nodded. "And an announcement." Theo turned out the lamp on her vanity table.

"Two weeks!"

"Two weeks and one day. The Betrothal Ball is on the twenty-fifth."

"I wish I could strangle him!"

"I wish so, too," Theo said pleasantly as she went to her bed. "But only if you could get away with it. Goodnight."

Maeve huffed. "How are you so calm?"

Theo climbed under the sheet and light blanket and pulled her knees up to hug them. "I am not altogether sure, but honestly, I feel nothing. Absolutely nothing."

The fact that the statement was true was the most frightening thing of all. Maeve left and closed the door before she allowed the tears of frustration to come.

Chapter Five

our days. Dab had enjoyed all of four days with his father before the pain was too much and Henry Adams was sedated to senselessness. On a muggy, overcast late morning, the thirteenth of August, Dab and his mother sat by his bedside in a silent vigil watching and listening to each of his father's labored breaths.

The breaths slowed.

Slowed.

And then … stopped.

Dab waited for the next one, but it didn't come. He looked at his mother. Her face was wet with tears, but she was calm, resigned. Her hand still held her husband's. They had known the end was imminent, so why was it bizarre when it arrived? It was so final.

"I'm sorry for your loss," the physician said from the door.

Dab hadn't realized the man was still there. He turned his head and nodded stiffly, and the doctor left with a soft stride.

"He will be prepared and then taken," Charlotte said quietly, not looking away from her husband's still face.

Dab had spent the last days with his father talking and playing chess or backgammon. He had spent little time with his mother. When he'd not been with his father, she had been. He'd heard nothing of arrangements.

"He did not want a funeral," she said.

"No funeral?"

"Not in a church. Nothing showy. He couldn't abide the thought."

Dab looked at his father again. He already looked different, somehow. Shrunken.

"He said death should not stop the living," she said with a wan smile. "He wanted me to promise not to stay in black for long. He didn't want the drapes drawn or a hatchment placed on the front door. I told him it wouldn't stay up for more than a few months, but there would be a mourning wreath."

How long had his father known he was dying? It made Dab feel ill to think about.

"No black arm bands for you," she said. "He wrote it all down. He had very particular ideas on the matter. On most things really. Oh, God, I miss him. Already. Isn't that strange?"

Dab shook his head. It wasn't strange at all.

She sniffed and wiped her eyes. "He left a list of those he wanted informed. He said all the others could learn about it in the newspaper." She sighed tiredly as she leaned back. "A few words spoken at the gravesite was all he wanted."

"He was ready," Dab realized aloud.

She nodded. "He was. Since you came, he was. And he is no longer in pain."

Dab lowered his head, unable to hold back the tears. He'd waited too long to forgive. He hated himself for that.

His mother rose. She leaned down and kissed her husband's forehead, pressed a hand to his still chest and left the room, touching her son's shoulder as she passed.

Dab gave in to the grief of loss and bitter regret. When it finally subsided, he sighed deeply and touched his father's arm. "I'm sorry," he mouthed. He leaned closer to whisper, as pointless as it was. "I will forgive her. I swear it."

He rose and left knowing the servants would want to say their goodbyes.

Dab sat cattycorner from his mother at dinner. She had changed into unrelieved black. The meal consisted of a simple consommé, bread and a green salad but neither of them had an appetite.

"Who is on the list?" Dab asked.

She looked up sharply, almost startled by his voice.

"To be informed," he added.

"His friends, Pratt, Bonneville, Reedley and a few others. His cousin, Ronald and his wife."

"Tabitha," Dab mused. "Isn't that her name?"

"Yes." She took a sip of wine. "I wouldn't have thought you'd remember that," she ventured.

"I have an excellent memory," he snapped. He was immediately sorry for it. "It's how I got through school, you know," he added in a lighter tone.

"Nonsense. You always had keen intelligence. You could say your ABCs and count to a hundred before you were four."

"A savant, then," he teased.

She smiled and they ate awhile in silence.

"I will forever be grateful to you," she uttered. "He was at peace because of you."

He shook his head. "I waited too long."

"He was at peace in the end because of you, Dabney. That is everything. The rest is history that cannot be changed. If it could have been changed, we would have done it long ago."

He moved the breadbasket closer to have something to focus on. "Who else is on the list?"

"Some of the neighbors. My sister, but she won't be able to make it in time."

He looked at her.

"The burial will be on Thursday morning," she said. "Before the heat of the days sets in."

"What about his brother?" he asked with an edge.

She shook her head. "They have been estranged since—"

He selected a piece of bread and began to tear it apart. He tore it into bits. He didn't want it. He just wanted to tear it apart. He didn't want anything except to be finished with the anger and bitterness he'd carried inside for too long. But how when it was so much a part of him? "I promised Father," he said without looking up at her. He paused, but she remained silent. He looked up at her. It looked as though she was holding her breath. "I would forgive you."

A single tear slipped down her face.

"I forgive you," he said.

She gasped and brought the napkin to her face. She nodded woodenly and then got up and left the room.

Done. It was done. And he had to mean it. They had all paid too much. He leaned back and drew in a breath. He exhaled, feeling better. Done. It was done. By God, he had to mean it this time.

<u>*Chapter Six*</u>

I absolutely *hate* him!" Laurel declared as she paced the parlour floor.

"More tea?" Theo asked her eldest sister, Cissy. The pair of them had come to talk her out of the engagement Hib was forcing on her. But it was a pointless endeavor, one she was bored stiff talking about. There was no way around it without them all suffering for it.

Cissy frowned at Theo. "You do *not* have to do this. Mamma and Papa would have never allowed it and you know it."

"Oh, Narcissus," Theo snapped. "It is only happening because they are gone. We have been over this." She sighed loudly. "Why didn't Greta come with you?"

Cissy looked uncomfortable. "She had a music lesson."

"Is that the only reason?" Theo asked. She'd hardly seen her younger sister since their father's passing.

"It's been hard on her," Cissy said sadly.

"I know that, but it's as if she's avoiding me. Does she fear I'm going to die, too?"

Cissy and Laurel exchanged a look and then Laurel returned to her chair. "Not anymore," Laurel replied. "She did fear it. We all did. Greta will fully recover, you know. In time. Hers were wounds of the heart, and those are always the slowest to heal. Frankly, we're far more worried about you."

"You needn't be. I will be fine. In fact, I will be wealthy, so I can help both of you."

Cissy huffed. "We do not need help. We need you to … come back to yourself and fight this thing. Either Laurel or I will happily make room for you."

Laurel nodded emphatically. "I'll put Danielle in with Molly and Hannah—"

"No."

"Then you'll come to us," Cissy said. "You and Gret can share her room."

"No."

Laurel smacked the arm of her chair in frustration.

"Darling," Cissy said to Theo. "You are not quite right since Papa's death."

It was true, so she could hardly argue the point or even resent it being said.

Cissy shook her head. "We cannot let you do this."

"I love you both. And I love our nosy Maeve," she said in a louder voice since Maeve was undoubtedly listening just beyond the door. "But this is my decision. Look at me. I am not upset."

"*That* is the problem," Laurel said.

"I think it's a good thing," Theo retorted.

"A good thing," Laurel repeated in astonishment. "That you're being forced out of here, the only place we have left that had anything to do with Mamma and Papa, and made to marry a man you don't even know because it holds some advantage to Hib? What's he getting out of it, anyway?"

Theo didn't know and it felt as if they were having the same conversation for the fourteenth time. "Would the two of you prefer me to be wailing and weeping, wringing my hands and shouting about how unfair it is?"

Cissy leaned forward. "The shouting part, yes."

"You are not really the wailing and wringing your hands sort," Laurel retorted. "What we would prefer is to make a plan and then collectively tell our cursed half-brother to go straight to hell."

"There is a plan, and it is this," Theo stated calmly. "Hib is sending his carriage for me tomorrow and I will be driven past the houses of the two contenders in case that moves me to a decision. Perhaps I'll like the brick or hedgerow of one better than the other. Then I will see Sir Amos Pearce again on Friday at some reception, and I will see Mr. Pugh at a ball on Saturday. Neither of them seems like ogres. I'm certain I could do worse." Her sisters shook their heads, clearly aggrieved. She felt badly for them.

"Where's the feeling, Theo?" Cissy fretted. "The emotion? One should have feelings when deciding whom one will marry."

In principle, it was true, of course. "I'm getting a bit of a headache," Theo said to end the visit.

"You are saying that because you want us to go," Laurel said suspiciously.

"No. Stay. Have more tea. Plot and scheme with Maeve to your hearts' content." She rose. "But I'm going to lie down. Give Greta my love?"

Cissy sighed. "Of course, I will."

"I want to see her. I need to see her. We were so close, and now—"

Laurel stood again. "Will you think about what we've said?"

Theo went closer and kissed her cheek. Next, she bent to kiss Cissy's, and then she left the room. She would not make assurances she could not keep.

Your Presence is Requested at

The Betrothal Ball

Woodley-Forester Hall   Curzon Street   Saturday the 25th inst.   Eight P.M.

The End of the Season hails new beginnings!

Chapter Seven

*D*ab met the fellows at White's on Saturday night, the twenty-fifth of August, for drinks and dinner before leaving to fetch their respective ladies for the Betrothal Ball, one of the big events of the season.
Tonight, was Dab's first social night out since his father's passing. He felt a bit strange and hollow, as if he were simply going through the motions.

His father's final days and his death had changed him. He couldn't have said precisely what was altered, but he felt more aware. More pensive. He didn't know what the future would hold, but changes were in store. He had given notice at Albany. He was giving up his set and moving back home where he would take over managing the estate, such as it was.

He would put one foot in front of the other and make his way. He would not pursue Cora. Perhaps he would never pursue any lady at all. He had the responsibility of the barony to think about now.

His mother had suffered with melancholy and utter inertia until the last few days when she'd gone into action. She'd stripped her husband's room of the bedcoverings, drapes and most of his personal possessions. She was giving all of it away. His clothing was being given away.

"Why?" Dab asked her one afternoon while he was perusing the items she'd set aside, thinking he might want them. "Why do this?"

"It helps," she replied with a light shrug. "Keeping busy. Saying goodbye to each thing. That may sound silly, but it doesn't feel it. Your father and I had more than thirty years together." She swallowed back a surge of emotion. "So there are many goodbyes to say."

He picked up a decorative compass he'd always liked. "Perhaps he can help me find my direction."

She smiled. "He had faith that you will find it, and so do I."

Things were carefully cordial between he and his mother and Dab wondered if it would ever be more than that. But a person could only take one step at a time, and he'd taken several these last weeks.

~~~

"Your cursed half-brother has arrived," Maeve announced from the door. "He and his troll of a wife are waiting in their fine carriage."

Theo was staring at her pale silver-blue gown in the mirror. She'd never worn anything finer. Hib had spent a tidy sum on new gowns, slippers and gloves in order to add to her appeal. The diamonds on her earlobes and around her neck were on loan from his wife, but Theo had rarely worn diamonds before.

Maeve came closer. "You look beautiful. I wish I could lock you in a closet!"

Theo smiled. "I know you do. Thank you for that."

"Very nice," Cyrus commented when she was helped into the carriage.

"Yes," his wife Mildred agreed with her usual expression of disdain.

Naturally, they were referring to her attire which they had paid for. Politeness demanded that she thank them for the compliments, but she couldn't bring herself to do it.

The carriage started forward. "So which of them will it be?" Cyrus asked.

"I am not certain."

He frowned. "The announcements are at midnight."

"I realize that."

"I need to tell them something before that," he snapped. "They are expecting an answer."

"I realize that as well."

"You've had time with both of them. Seen their houses. I gave you a grasp of their financial standing. You are fortunate to be in this position."

"Yes," Mildred agreed. "You are."

Theo refused to look at her. "Marriage is a big decision. I don't even know them yet. Not really."

Cyrus leaned forward. "I will give you exactly two hours to tell me which of them you choose, or I will choose for you." He paused and narrowed his eyes at her, but she didn't reply or look away. "Ten o'clock," he thundered, causing her to jump slightly.

She looked out the window, despising him with all her being. "What do you think our father would say about this?"

He sat back. "I don't give a damn."

"No," she agreed. "You never did, did you?"

"Not since the day he chose a new family over the old."

Mildred reached over to pat his hand.

Theo hated both of them. "Your mother died before there was another family," she reminded him.

"Another family he *preferred*!"

There was no point in debating her father's sentiments. Cyrus would never let go of his grudge, reasonable or not. "He was as good of a father as you would allow," she added, unable to stop herself.

"It hardly matters. He is dead and gone. Dust to dust."

It was said with relish, which sent a shot of anguish through her. "Ten o'clock, Theodora. And not one minute later."

Mr. Pugh wedged in first thing and asked for a dance. Theo complied. Cyrus and Mildred watched her the entire time probably concerned that she would emulate the fictional Cinderella and make a mad dash for home before midnight. And she might have, except where would she go?

"Tonight is the night," Pugh commented as she sipped punch after the dance. He was having claret. "I hear there are eight engagements to be announced so far," he said. "How many will there be by midnight do you think?"

"I have no idea."

"Are you nervous?"

"A little," she admitted. And it was true. Her emotions had been muffled for weeks upon weeks, or even longer, but some very unpleasant ones were steadily rising to the surface and breaking open like bubbles on boiling water. Fear, dread, frustration. "I have never enjoyed being the center of attention."

He grinned. "I have always enjoyed it."

She could well imagine that. She rather liked the man. "Mr. Pugh, may I ask," she began hesitantly.

"Yes, you may," he quipped.

"I am wondering … why you?"

"Why me?"

"I think you know my brother presented me with two men for consideration."

"Yes."

"Why are you one of them? Does he owe you money? Or a favor?"

He studied her. "Does it matter?"

She considered how to reply. Was it simple curiosity on her part? The answer, if he provided one, did not change a thing. "I am asking," she said levelly. "So, I would hope you would assume it does matter."

He signaled to a waiter for another drink. "Yes. He owes me."

"Money," she said quietly.

He nodded.

"And my dowry—"

He smiled. "Does not nearly cover the debt, but I am willing to forgive the rest. If I am fortunate enough to acquire your fair hand."

The sentiment was flattering and she appreciated his honesty. "Thank you for telling me."

"You are lovely and desirable, Theodora. I can see the intelligence and wit in those eyes of yours."

She felt herself blush and pointedly looked away.

"Do you find compliments difficult to abide?"

"A bit." She looked at him again.

He sobered. "You are also tender and a bit wounded still. I know about the loss of your parents, and I know how difficult that can be to get beyond. I find myself responding to all of it, wanting to protect you. I will be a good husband," he said, edging closer, his gaze intense. "Say that you choose me."

His words were affecting. "I see why you are a good businessman, sir."

"Because I am persuasive? Charming? Add irresistible to that list and you will make me the happiest man at this ball."

She smiled and noticed Sir Amos approaching. "Sir Amos," she said under her breath.

He frowned.

"Miss Martel," Sir Amos said with a slight bow when he reached her.

"Sir Amos," she returned. "Good evening."

The two men exchanged a look of dislike.

"May I have the next dance?" Sir Amos asked.

She looked at Charles Pugh who was none too happy about having her filched. "Will you excuse me, Mr. Pugh?"

"If I must, Miss Martel." He tipped his head in acceptance before giving Sir Amos a black look.

On and on it went as the night wore on, both men trying to monopolize her. She'd never been so relieved to have a complete stranger ask her for a dance. She had an urge to take his arm and run him to the dance floor.

By nine thirty, her nervousness had given way to such acute anxiety that she felt nauseated. She slipped away to find a retiring room, fearful she might be sick to her stomach.

Dab stood in the immense ballroom with his friends, and with his back to Cora Palmes who now stood some ten or twelve yards away. She had steadily been making her way closer to him. He had tried to make it appear that he had not seen her. He had no wish to hurt her feelings, but nor did he have a desire to waste time on pointless chit chat, especially when it only served to encourage her. He also did not want to encourage the spies and writers of papers and scandal rags. They always seemed to be watching.

"So theatrical," Jonathan remarked, staring at the stage along one wall. It was framed with white curtains and decorated with bows, frills, flowers and a large cutout of wedding bells. Engagements would be announced there tonight with great pageantry.

Dab nodded. "It is, that. Does it make you want to step up and announce something?"

"If the lady would say yes, I would happily do it."

The others chuckled. Jonathan was in love with Lakely Walston, Nigel's younger sister, and she was in love with him, but not yet ready to consent to matrimony. The way she saw it, Jonathan had ignored her for years. Yes, he had been unaware of her feelings, not to mention bound by a code of honor amongst his closest friends, but she did not care. Lakely was beautiful and spirited. One did not ignore her if she did not wish it.

"What about you, Lord Sonden?" Hugh asked Dab playfully. "One cannot help noticing poor Miss Palmes pining for you across the room."

JG started to look around to see.

"Don't look, damn it," Dab scolded. "I don't want her knowing I'm aware of it."

JG gave him a dour look. "I seem to recall you saying something about liking the idea of marrying an heiress," he retorted.

The others grinned and nodded.

"So do I," Nigel said. "I remember it very well."

"I suppose you would," Jonathan jumped in." Since it was your wife he was talking about."

"Before he'd even met her," Dab stated. "And I was joking."

"Oh," JG laughed. "You were joking."

Dab rolled his eyes. "If you *gentlemen* will excuse me, I need a smoke."

"We'll stop," Hugh said. He sniffed. "After I mention that Miss Palmes's father seems to be pining for the match with the same fervor as his daughter. It seems you have charmed them both."

Dab turned and left his friends enjoying themselves at his expense. Not that he wouldn't be right there with them if the shoe was on the other foot.

Theo went up the stairs and down the side of the hall that was not cordoned off. The rooms available for ladies' use each had a ribbon tied on the doorknob. If the door was shut, the room was in use. She passed three closed doors and went into the fourth. She shut the door and leaned against it. She had no doubt that Mildred would soon be coming for her. She and Cyrus had not taken their eyes off her all evening.

Theo went to the open door to the balcony and stepped outside taking gulps of air. She moved to the edge and looked down. If she jumped and died, she hoped the newspapers would read, '*Woman jumps to her death to thwart her feckless toad of a half-brother who was trying to force an unwanted marriage on her!*'

She turned around knowing that she could not merely hide here. Mildred would be coming, and she would happily drag her out. Theo stepped back into the room, paced, and then went back to the door and opened it.

"Theodora?" Mildred called from close by.

Theo took a step back. She started to shut the door again but, on second thought, she dashed over and ducked behind an upholstered chair. If Mildred saw the door open and the room empty, hopefully she would keep going. Theo held her breath and waited. She heard footsteps stop in the doorway and then walk on. A moment later, she heard Mildred call her name again.

Theo shook all over. She was nauseous. And how ridiculous did she look? What if someone came in to use the room and then screamed from fright to see her hiding there? How she wanted to run away from this house! Run and run. Returning to Dover and living in Spinster House, Maeve's family home, was not a bad idea at all. Not if Greta would go, too. If only her younger sister was not avoiding her as if she was a carrier of a plague.

"Excuse me," Mildred said from down the hall.

Theo's breath caught.

"Are there retiring rooms downstairs?"

"No," came the answer. "There are privy rooms downstairs, but the retiring rooms are all up here."

"I see. Did you happen to see a young woman in a silver blue gown in the last few minutes?"

"I have not, my lady."

"Thank you," Mildred replied curtly.

Theo listened to her footfalls as Mildred walked by the room again. Slowly, Theo stood and gripped the back of the chair, her mind racing. What was she to do? What could she do?

Dab walked down the corridor past doors to verandas that ran along the side of the home. Some of the verandas were occupied by couples who did not appear to wish for additional company, but the third from the end had only a single occupant, a middle-aged gentleman smoking a cigar. "May I join you?" Dab asked.

"Of course," the man said with a friendly smile. "If the smell doesn't bother you."

"Not at all. I've even been known to partake."

"Care for one now?" The man asked patting his coat pocket. "I brought a few."

"No, thank you. I really just wanted to get away from my friends for a few moments."

"Having a go at you, are they?"

Dab chuckled. "They are."

"With good reason?"

Dab shrugged and then nodded. "I suppose. Which doesn't make it less annoying."

The man laughed. "Turner," he said, offering his hand. "Albert Turner."

Dab shook the hand. "Dabney Adams."

"What do you think of this business tonight, Adams?"

"It is more flamboyant than I would care for if I were having an engagement announced."

Albert Turner nodded. "The great lords and ladies are trying any gimmick these days to get us packed in." The man puffed on his cigar. "It tickles my wife." He looked over as a middle-aged woman joined them. "Speaking of which."

"There you are," she said pleasantly.

"My dear, this is Mr. Adams." He gestured to his wife. "My wife, Mary."

Dab bowed his head. "Mrs. Turner."

"Mr. Adams," she returned. Like her husband, she was slightly overweight with an easy, friendly manner. "You're not hiding from your bride to be, are you?"

He smiled. "No. There is no such lady."

She turned to her husband. "I have won the bet."

"Have you? Which bet is that?"

"There are nearly *six* hundred here."

"Ah." He looked at Dab. "She has a knack of guessing the number of guests." He looked back at his wife. "I don't recall it being a bet, though."

"You said there were perhaps four hundred in attendance, I said five, so clearly I win. And so far, a dozen engagements will be announced."

"I can hardly wait," her husband returned drolly. He offered his wife the cigar and she took it and had a puff before handing it back.

"You are a remarkably handsome fellow," Mary said to Dab. "And not married yet?"

Hopefully, they didn't have an unmarried daughter lurking about. "I am not," he replied.

Albert Turner's grin stayed in place. "I warn you, Adams, she enjoys pairing up anyone who ventures into her path."

"I was merely asking," she defended herself. "Trying to get to know Mr. Adams here." She cocked her head. "Dabney Adams?"

Dab nodded. "Yes."

Her husband looked at her with surprise.

She chuckled. "The papers call him Adonis," she explained. "I see why now."

"Adonis, eh?" The cigar had gone out and Albert put it on the railing. The people on another veranda burst into laughter, and the three of them glanced that way.

"What do your parents think of all the hullabaloo about you?" Mary asked.

Answering questions about his parents had been uncomfortable for years. "My father died quite recently."

Her face fell. "Oh, I am sorry."

Albert murmured, his expression one of sympathy.

"He saw the humor in it, though," Dab added.

"I will freely admit that I read the tripe," Mary said. "But I always wonder how the parents of those being written about feel. If it's flattering, that's all well and good, but if it's mean spirited, that's another matter. Although it's never mean spirited about you that I recall."

"No. Snarky, perhaps. Intrusive. I've often wondered who these people are. Where do they come up with what they write?"

Mary nodded.

"I'll go fetch more drinks," Albert said. He looked at Dab. "What are you having?"

"Anything but punch or lemonade."

"It should have a kick to it, eh?"

"My friends were saying I could use one," Dab jested.

Albert grinned as he started out, practically colliding with a pretty woman. "I beg your pardon, Miss," he apologized.

"No, no, no," she said quickly. She glanced behind her, as nervous as could be. "It was my fault." She glanced behind her again and then stepped out on the veranda. "May I join you?" she asked breathlessly.

Her angst was so high, it robbed them all of the power of speech.

She didn't wait for an answer but stepped around Dab and backed against the corner of the wall. "For a moment?" she stammered just above a whisper.

"Are you alright?" Mary asked her worriedly.

"No," she whispered.

Albert looked down the hall and back at her. "Avoiding a burly man in a dark red waistcoat?"

"Yes," she admitted.

She was shaking all over. Her breath was ragged. Dab stepped in front of her to hide her. "You were saying?" he said to Mary.

"Yes. What I said to him was … that was not seemly at all," she declared, speaking more loudly than before. "But did he listen to me?" She paused as the burly man stopped in the door scowling darkly. He poked his head out to see the occupants before striding on without uttering a word. They all listened to his footsteps.

"He'll be going on to the next one," Albert warned.

Each veranda was in clear sight of the ones around it, so Dab changed places with the lady, attempting to block her from view of the next.

Mary stepped closer to her. "You are trembling like a leaf. Is that man a villain?"

Villain was a ridiculous word, but Dab felt an equally ridiculous urge to reach out and physically support the young woman.

"Yes," she uttered. "And also my half-brother."

"Oh, dear," Mary replied. "Why is he after you?"

Albert cleared his throat. "He's on the next one, looking around the grounds," he warned quietly.

"He is forcing an engagement on me," she whispered. "He wants it announced tonight."

"He's gone now," Albert said. "Change places again."

The girl stepped behind Dab as Mary prattled on, "But why she would have chosen to wear that particular shade is beyond me," she voiced, looking to catch another glimpse of the half-brother.

"Yes," Albert agreed. "Beyond me, as well. It was a most disagreeable colour." The brother walked by again. Albert waited a few moments and peeked out. "He's gone for now," he reported.

Dab turned to face the lady. Mary also stepped closer and Albert came to stand between Dab and his wife forming a protective, if somewhat comical looking wall.

"He cannot force you. Can he?" Mary asked.

The young woman was slender and pretty. The half-brother had been tall and stocky. He'd looked nothing like her.

"He thinks he can," she replied. "I cannot see much of a way around it."

"Who is he?" Dab asked.

She looked at him. "His name is Cyrus Martel. He recently became Viscount Chausterforth."

Dab did not know any Chausterforth. "Recently became?"

She nodded. "Since my father passed on."

"I'm sorry," he said. "Mine passed recently, as well."

"It is a terrible loss," she said thickly. "I am sorry for yours."

In the lantern light, her eyes looked golden. A pretty woman, a damsel in distress, with golden eyes. No wonder he felt like donning medieval armor and calling for a white steed.

Albert spoke. "What does your mother have to say about him attempting to force you?"

"She died three months before my father. There was … an accident."

"You poor thing," Mary cried. "Have you any family you can turn to?"

"I do, but none that can help. I have two older sisters and a younger sister. I also have family in Dover, but none that can help. He sold our house, you see."

"Your half-brother?" Mary asked.

She nodded.

"What is your name, dear?" Mary asked kindly.

"Theo. Theodora Martel," she corrected herself. "I apologize for bursting in on you like I did." She said, looking around at all of them.

Mary shook her head and waved off the apology. "I am Mary Turner, and this is my husband, Bert."

Bert nodded his head to her. "Pleased to meet you, Theo."

"And this is Mr. Adams," Mary continued. "Dabney Adams."

"It's nice to meet you all," Theo replied.

She hadn't shown an inkling of recognition at his name. "Are you from Dover?" Dab asked.

"Yes. I am not a stranger to London exactly. We have always come here for a few months in the spring."

"For the Season," Mary said.

"I suppose. None of us were ever involved, really."

"With your father a viscount?" Mary asked, cocking her head in confusion.

Theo smiled sadly. "Papa used to say his title was written on paper, and *that* was about what it was worth. We never minded. We really never even noticed. Our lives were in Dover, except for the trips here when we'd each get a few new gowns and attend the theatre and symphony and enjoy a ball or two. But nothing like this or the ones I've attended these last few weeks."

The last few weeks, Dab mused. When he had not been attending. Bert walked over to look in the corridor and then resumed his place.

"So your mother died in an accident," Mary said, summing up what they'd learned. "And a mere three months later, your father died, as well. Was it a result of the same accident?"

"Mary," Bert chided gently. "Theo may not want to discuss it."

"It's alright," Theo said. "No. It wasn't the same accident. It was his heart."

Mary nodded. "And then your half-brother inherited everything?"

"Yes. That wasn't supposed to happen but, when she died, everything of my mother's went to my father. No one ever expected that. She was much younger than he."

"So the brother sold your family home in Dover?" Mary asked.

"Yes. And now he is selling our townhome. Because he can. He always resented my mother. And my father, once he married my mother. He never gave two thoughts to my sisters or myself."

"But now you are vulnerable," Dab realized.

She seemed to consider the question. "I have very little money of my own and no income. I am soon to be without a home, so I suppose I am."

"All for money," Mary said disdainfully.

"And Cyrus married into money," Theo exclaimed. "I think it's also about … power and revenge. Although apparently, he's acquired debt. That's why the two particular gentlemen were chosen."

"Two gentlemen?" Dab repeated.

"I was given a choice. They are both here tonight, waiting for me to say which of them it is to be."

Mary touched the girl's arm. "I have an idea. Why don't we sneak you out of here?"

"You're so kind, but I have nowhere to go."

"What about your sisters?" Mary asked.

Theo shook her head. "They have neither the room nor the resources, although they are willing. They would rather I do that. They have all but begged. But I will not do that to them."

Mary lifted her chin. "Then you shall come to our home," she stated.

Theo didn't reply for a moment, she seemed so taken aback. "I … I couldn't but thank you."

"You would be welcome," Bert said gently. "We have the room."

Dab found himself hoping she would agree.

"Theodora, it is a man's world," Mary declared. "We ladies have to band together when we can." She gave her husband an affectionate smile. "We ladies and good husbands."

Bert grinned. "Thank you for making me an exception, my dear."

"You are the exception. And there are good men, as well," Mary said to Dab.

Dab inclined his head. "Thank you for making *me* an exception." Out of the corner of his eye, he saw Theo looking at him inquisitively. He turned to her. "What do you want to do, Miss Martel? The three of us are at your disposal."

She was at a loss. "I don't know," she admitted. "Honestly, I didn't plan to make a run for it. I just … did."

"Who does he want you to marry?" Dab asked curiously. "You said he had debt. Does he owe these men?"

"Yes, I believe so. I know he owes Mr. Pugh, because I asked, and he told me. I don't know about Sir Amos Pearce. Do you know them?"

"No," Dab replied.

"I don't mean to say anything against them," Theo said. "They do not strike me as bad men. Though I hardly know them well enough to consider marriage."

"Then why not escape?" Dab challenged. "At least, for tonight. It will buy you time."

"Because if I do, Cyrus will choose," she replied. "The engagement will be announced with or without me. I wouldn't really be buying anything. Except of course his wrath."

"No, Theo, you're mistaken," Mary rejoined with a shake of her head. "The presentations this evening are going to be quite orchestrated."

Theo looked at her with held breath.

"She would know," Albert interjected. "She made it a point to find out."

"You noticed the stage, of course," Mary rushed on.

Theo nodded.

"Each lady will be escorted up one side of it by a footman, who then steps away as the master of ceremonies announces her. Next, her betrothed is announced …from the card she hands the footman." Mary paused to make sure Theo understood. "The master of ceremonies has a list of the ladies only."

"So if I am not there," Theo said softly.

"The announcement will not happen," Mary stated. "It's only once the man's name is called that he comes up and joins her on stage. They then exit through the back, the curtains pulling apart for them."

A shaky sigh escaped Theo. She smiled with relief and excitement, if Dab was not mistaken. "So is it to be escape?" he asked hopefully.

She nodded. "Yes!"

Mary grinned. "Wonderful. She'll be put in our carriage and sent home. We'll send word to the housekeeper."

"Can't we go, as well?" Bert pouted.

"No! I want to see the show."

"I am so grateful," Theo said to Mary.

The ladies clasped hands. "I have always wanted a daughter to dote on. The housekeeper's name is Vera, and she'll take good care of you."

"I am grateful to all of you," Theo said, looking at the men with a shy smile that did something strange to Dab's heart.

He felt an unreasonable thrill. "The only question is how we get you out of here," he said. "Shall we escort you down the corridor and out the front doors? Or I can lift you over the railing and we can sneak around to the front."

Mary chortled. "That sounds more fun."

"And safer," Theo said. "But I don't need you to lift me. Did I not mention I'm not really a lady?" She turned, put her hand on the railing and hopped over it.

Mary made a little squeal. "Oh, I adore her," she declared, clapping her hands together.

"I'll meet you around front," Bert called to Theo, who was already hurrying on.

"Wait for me," Dab said to Theo. He hopped over the railing and followed her.

"I'll see you at home," Mary called with delight in her voice.

Chapter Eight

*T*heo turned back to Dab. "You don't have to, Mr. Adams. Really. I've already taken up your time."

"This is the most fun I've had at any ball in I don't remember when," he returned. "My friends call me Dab, by the way."

Good Lord, he was so handsome. She had never seen anyone as handsome. And he was kind. He took the lead and she followed. She couldn't believe she was running away, but it was better than the alternative. She felt high with elation. When had she last felt that? "I have to get word to Maeve," she realized aloud.

He stopped and turned back to her. "Who is Maeve?"

"She was my mother's maid. She is like a beloved aunt to us. She's at the house."

"I'll get word to her. I'm sure she could come to you."

She shook her head. "She must remain blameless. Cyrus is spiteful."

"Then I'll explain what's happened. What's the address?"

"Fifteen Barton Street. It has a dark blue door."

He nodded. "I'll go there once I see you safely away."

"But you'll miss the party."

"I could not care less about it."

She felt an urge to cry from gratitude. "Thank you."

He smiled. "May I come see you tomorrow?"

Her heart was beating in an unnatural rhythm. Why couldn't this glorious man have been one of her brother's choices?

"Then I can tell you what she said," he added.

Ah. Of course. He was merely a good man on an errand that he would see to its conclusion. "I would appreciate that." He walked on again and she followed.

As they neared the front of the house, he slowed, looked around and then turned back to her. "Stay here and I'll find Bert."

47

She nodded and he walked on.

Theo twiddled her fingers nervously and chewed on her bottom lip as she waited. How many minutes had it been? It probably hadn't been five, but it felt like more. She glanced around and then behind her. A man, a stranger, was striding toward her. He was some distance away and yet he seemed to be looking right at her.

He *was* looking at her.

She swallowed hard as she went in the direction Dab had gone. She did not see him, but another man was looking at her in a hard way. Cyrus had sent them. She just knew it. She veered away from him and went toward the line of parked carriages, but he was faster.

"Miss Martel," he said just before he gripped her arm. "You seem to be lost."

The other man was also closing in. "I am not lost! Unhand me."

"I'm afraid I can't do that." His grip tightened hard enough to bruise her arm as he began walking her back, despite her resistance. The other man stayed on her opposite side, ready to grab her if needed. How humiliating! People were looking. She considered screaming. She could pretend to faint. But no. One of them would just pick her up and carry her in. She looked around for Dab but did not see him anywhere.

Already, they had reached the front steps to the portico. Dozens of guests stood around, but would any of them help her if she cried out? She was being forced up the steps. She drew breath to scream but froze when she saw Cyrus as he emerged from the house.

"There you are," he said. He strode purposefully for her. "They need you," he said. His voice was cheerful, his expression calm, but he was inwardly seething. She could sense it. She could see it in his eyes. He took hold of her arm with an even harder grip than the first man. She would be left with bruises. "What are you doing?" he said under his breath as he marched her in.

"I was getting a breath of fresh air. Let go of me. You are hurting my arm."

They went through the grand foyer. "You are not so foolish as to think you can run away from this?"

"I was not running away from anything! I was taking the air because I felt unwell. Then these men closed in on me. Now let go of me!"

In the corridor, he shoved her into an alcove and whipped her around to face him. "I have secured the necessary documents for you to be married tomorrow," he threatened quietly. "To either man. Give me anymore difficulty, and I will turn you over to one of them tonight to enjoy his husbandly privileges a day early."

She drew in a shaky breath knowing he meant it. He would do it. She would be shoved into a carriage, maybe kicking and screaming, but forced nonetheless, and delivered to his choice of a husband. "Which is it?" she asked coldly. "Which of them do you want me to marry?"

He narrowed his eyes, and finally let go of her. "It is still your choice, Theodora." He handed over both men's calling cards. "It's only the announcement that needs to happen tonight. You can have a month until the wedding. You can have a gown made. Your husband will have a trousseau made for you."

She was close to tears, but she would hold them back. He would not wring them from her.

"Whom do you favor?" he asked, trying to sound reasonable.

"I am torn," she replied flatly. Which was true. It felt as if she was being slowly ripped in two like an unwanted paper doll.

"Your name is fourth on the list," he stated. "I would prefer to know ahead of time and be able to prepare them, but you have only until they call your name to decide. Do you understand?"

"It is not complicated," she retorted. "What might I fail to understand?"

He smiled viciously. "You're so clever, aren't you?"

She did not reply.

"Fail me in this," he said softly. "And I will have you removed from here and I will beat you bloody before turning you over to Sir Amos. He is my choice."

"Meaning you owe even more money to him than to Pugh," she said with disdain.

He glowered and then yanked her out of the alcove and onward. He walked her to a closed door, cordoned off for brides-to-be only. "This is Miss Martel," he said to the footman manning the door.

The man checked the list and then looked at her. "Do you have the card of your fiancé?"

She wanted to shake Cyrus's hand off her arm. Could the footman not see she was being coerced? "I do."

He opened the door for her. "Welcome and congratulations."

She stepped into the room, a spacious salon. The six or seven young women in the room all looked over at her. They seemed anxious, but happy. Precisely how a bride-to-be should look if they weren't trapped and powerless. She felt like weeping and perhaps screaming.

Bert had located their carriage, spoken to the driver, and was headed back when Dab reached him. "Should I have him go back around and pick her up on that side?" Bert asked. "He's at the far end over here."

Dab thought about it. If they did that, they risked the carriage getting stuck in traffic. Latecomers were still arriving, and other carriages circled because there was not sufficient room to park. "No," Dab replied. "I'll walk her to the carriage."

Bert nodded. "Then he can pull right out and go."

"And the only risk is her being sighted as we make our way there. I suppose her brother's driver might see us, but we won't stop no matter what."

Bert nodded. "You get her, and I'll watch from here and show you the way."

"It's a plan," Dab said with a grin before turning back to get Theo. He hadn't gone a dozen feet when he saw her being roughly escorted up the front steps by two men. Her brother was coming toward her as well.

"Oh, no," Bert said, coming up behind him. "They got her!"

Dab stared in disbelief. Martel had men there? Spying on her? What was this business of marrying her off really about? What did he have on the line?

"What are we going to do now?" Bert asked.

"I don't know," Dab admitted. What could they do?

Dab found Jonathan, Lakely and her sister Ada pretty much where he'd left his group of friends. "Where are the others?" he asked.

The three looked at him, baffled by his intensity.

"They are dancing or having refreshments," Jonathan replied. "Were they supposed to keep us informed of their whereabouts?"

"What is wrong with you?" Lakely asked Dab.

"I met someone," he began. "It's a long story, but she—"

Lakely cocked her head. *She?*

"She is being forced to marry someone," he continued. "The engagement is to be announced tonight. Her half-brother has arranged it and insists upon it."

"Uh," Jonathan said. "You just met this lady and learned all this … in the last half hour?"

Dab was looking around. "I don't know how long ago it was," he said distractedly.

"Since you left for a smoke?" Jonathan asked.

"Who are you looking for?" Lakely asked.

"Her! Theo."

"Her name is Theo?" Ada asked.

"Theodora Martel. I just passed her brother. He's over there looking smug. I wanted to punch his face. Where are they putting the ladies to be announced?"

"A room has been provided for their use," Lakely replied. "The salon next door, as a matter of fact. Why? Are you planning to smuggle her out?"

"I tried smuggling her out earlier, but they grabbed her when I was finding the carriage."

Jonathan gawked at the answer, and he was not the only one, but then he looked at Lakely, having experienced a new thought. "How do you know where the ladies are? Are you thinking of joining them?"

"Hardly."

"It would be alright with me."

"Dab," she said, ignoring Jonathan. "What happened with Theo?"

"Actually," Jonathan said. "I'm wondering what happened to my friend, Dabney Adams. He was here earlier. Then he went to have a smoke and *this* fellow showed up in his place. I will admit he looks like Dab, but—"

Lakely gave Jonathan an irritated frown. "Jonathan! Do you mind?"

Ada stepped closer to Dab. "Can we help?"

"It would help to understand what happened after you left," Lakely stated impatiently.

"I went to a veranda where a man was smoking," Dab said. "We got talking and his wife joined us. Incredibly nice people, Bert and Mary Turner. He was about to go get more drinks for us when Theo practically collided with him. He apologized and she apologized, and then she stepped out to join us, very nervous and, well, needing to hide. So we hid her. It had no sooner been managed then along came her half-brother searching for her. Once he'd gone on, we got the story."

"What is the story?" Ada asked.

"She's from Dover. She hasn't spent much time here. She had no idea who I was."

Lakely nearly rolled her eyes. "Everyone knows who you are."

He shook his head. "She didn't. There wasn't the merest flicker of recognition at my name."

Ada gave her sister a look. "I fail to see how that's important." She looked at Dab. "Go on."

"She lost her mother in an accident and her father three months after that. The estate went to her half-brother, who obviously does not care about her. He sold their family home in Dover and now he is selling the townhouse on Barton Street."

"You learned a good deal in a short time," Jonathan marveled.

"The problem," Dab continued. "Is that there's no money. She has elder sisters who have offered to take her in, but it would be a hardship on them, and she refuses to do it."

"But can he really force her to marry?" Ada asked.

"That is the question," Dab mused. "He is adamant. I saw that much. He has men here tonight who forced her back into the house when we were trying to get away."

"Oh, my," Ada breathed. "Why does he want it so badly?"

"It's always about money," Lakely stated.

Dab nodded in agreement. "It is."

"Who is she to marry?" Jonathan asked.

"There are two men she can choose from. Mr. Pugh and Sir Amos Pearce."

"It's just to be the announcement tonight?" Lakely asked, thinking aloud.

"Yes," Dab replied.

"Well then, if worse comes to worst, it could be announced, and we could still find her a way to get out of it tomorrow … or soon."

"Once it's been announced?" Ada asked. "It will be in the papers. Publicized. At that point, pride is on the line. And probably obligation."

"But not legal obligation," Lakely argued. "Not from the lady. Not unless there is a contract in place. People do break engagements. It's frowned on, but they do it."

Ada was trying to recall something. "Who was sued for breach of contract to marry last year?" she asked quietly.

"What is she like?" Lakely asked Dab. They had known him a long time and she had never seen him agitated with concern over a lady. One he'd met within the last hour, no less.

"She is—" Dab began

The three others shared a bemused look.

"She is pretty. Very nice." He sighed and looked around, clearly hoping to see her.

"I never thought I would see this," Jonathan remarked with a smirk.

Dab frowned. "What?"

"Nothing. Never mind."

"I'm going to go find the salon," Dab said.

"They will not let you in," Lakely rejoined. "It is exclusively for the betrothed ladies."

He huffed and walked off as Hugh rejoined them.

"It's too hot for dancing," Hugh complained. His face was flushed from it. "I think men should be allowed to use fans."

Ada opened hers and fanned him.

"You are an angel," Hugh said, leaning into it.

"You just missed Dab," Jonathan said. "I do believe he is thinking about proposing."

Hugh chuckled. "Because of the ribbing we gave him? I think not."

Lakely looked at Jonathan. "I think he might do if he could find a way," she agreed.

"Don't be absurd," Hugh said. "He is not the smallest bit enamored with Miss Palmes."

"Not her," Ada said with a shake of her head.

Hugh frowned with confusion.

"If I didn't know better," Jonathan said. "I would swear Cupid had been stalking him, followed him out to the veranda, took careful aim, and shot his arrow the instant Dab saw Theo."

"Who?" Hugh asked. "What?"

Jonathan chuckled and started to repeat the story, so Lakely stepped away and went after Dab. He could not get into the salon, but perhaps she could. To accomplish what, she did not know, but she'd never seen Dab in such a state. She found him pacing in the corridor.

"You're right," he said. "They won't even allow a message through."

"It's possible I can get in," she offered.

He stopped short. "Would you?"

"And say what?"

He looked at a loss. "I don't know, but she must feel so alone. I wish we could have gotten her away." He reached into his pocket and pulled out a card. "Give her this."

Lakely glanced at it and then stared at him.

Dab shrugged. "If she chooses to use it, it will buy time if nothing else."

If nothing else? "I know that you know this, Lord Sonden," she warned. "But if she chooses to use it and then backs out, or if you do, there will be a scandal."

"It's hers to use if she wishes. We'll handle whatever happens next together."

He had met the girl less than an hour ago and yet he was utterly in earnest. "I'll see what I can do," she said.

"Thank you, Lakely."

As she walked to the footman manning the door of the salon, she wondered if Jonathan hadn't been onto something when he'd maintained that Dab left their group earlier and returned as someone else. She couldn't wait to meet Theo.

The footman smiled at her. "Hello. Are you on the list?"

She gave her most charming smile. "I am. I am—" she leaned in and he did the same, probably allowing his gaze to roam where it oughtn't. "That one," she said, touching a name.

He looked back into her gaze. "Do you have the card of your intended?"

"Of course." She lifted the card Dab had just passed over.

"Welcome," he said languorously. He opened the door for her. "And congratulations. Miss—"

She couldn't recall the name she'd pointed to, so she flashed a smile. "Thank you," she said as she stepped past him. *One, two, three, four, five six*, Lakely counted the ladies inside. There were nine in the room, most of them chatting amongst themselves. One stood alone at the window. She had light brown hair with a fair amount of gold mixed in. Her gown was a pale silvery blue. Lakely started toward her. "Theo?" she asked when she reached her.

The girl looked at her with wide, amber eyes. "Yes."

She was pretty. Very pretty. There was a gripping innocence about her that made Lakely understand Dab's attraction. Theodora

Martel seemed different than most debutantes who were practiced in cool composure, poise at all costs, and the art of flirtation. "I'm Lakely Walston. I am a friend of Dab's."

"Oh," Theo said breathily, and her eyes filled. "He was so kind. They were all so kind to me. I was trying to get away, he was helping me, but a man grabbed me. Two men."

Lakely nodded. "Dab saw it. Are you alright?"

"Yes, but I fear I am thoroughly stuck. I would have jumped out this window and run for my life except his men are down there."

"Are they?" Lakely asked peering out the window. Indeed, she saw a man watching them. He had the audacity to wave at her. She narrowed her eyes at him and turned away. "Unbelievable," she said. "It appears your half-brother is taking no chances."

Theo studied her. "Dab explained?"

"Yes. And he gave me this to give to you."

Theo took the proffered card and looked at it, clearly startled. "I … don't understand."

"You have to hand over the card of your fiancé, do you not?"

Theo looked at her. She did not appear to be breathing.

"It will buy time if nothing else," Lakely reasoned.

Theo looked at the card again. "Lord Sonden?"

Lakely nodded. "Dab acquired the baronage when his father died a few weeks ago."

Theo looked at her searchingly. "I didn't realize it had been that recent." She paused. "He is your friend."

"Yes. He is a close friend of my brother, Nigel. They've been friends since they were boys. Dab didn't have the happiest family life, so he spent several summers and holidays with us. So, yes, he became a friend of mine as well."

"I see," Theo said softly.

"Do you care for either of the gentlemen your brother has proposed?"

"I hardly know them."

"They must realize that," Lakely mused. "Meaning either they think they are so charming they can win you over or... they don't much care."

Theo nodded slowly.

A lady with a list in hand and a frown on her face tapped Lakely on the shoulder. "I beg your pardon, Miss, but who did you say you were?"

"I don't believe I did. I am not actually supposed to be here, so I'd best be on my way." She gave Theo a reassuring nod and then left. Outside the room, the footman gawked at her; she'd probably gotten him into a spot of trouble. She considered apologizing but walked on. Dab waited at the end of the corridor. "I spoke with her," she said when she reached him. "She has the card."

"Did she say what she would do?" he asked anxiously.

"No. She was surprised and moved by it, though. There is something … lovely and blameless about her, isn't there?"

"Yes."

"I don't think she's prepared for this society of piranhas."

"And yet she has survived a lot," he said. "But she shouldn't be in this situation for the gain of her brother. Half-brother. Half-jackal," he added bitterly.

"There's nothing else that can be done," Lakely said. "But, at least, she knows there are others that care."

"Thank you," he said humbly.

"You're welcome."

Theo watched Miss Walston leave as did most of the others in the room. Her beauty was unparalleled, and her confidence was inspiring. Theo looked down at the calling cards. Soon, she would be led onto the stage in front of everyone where her decision would be announced.

She turned back to the window, shuffled the cards in her hand without looking at them and issued a prayerful plea to make the right selection. She looked down at the cards. Sir Amos was on top. She thought back on their earlier conversation when she'd gotten up the nerve to ask what her brother owed him. His reply had been that it was men's business and there was no need to worry her pretty little head about it.

Pretty little head indeed. What an annoying phrase. Her parents had discussed everything and decided important matters together. She could not imagine her father making such a statement to her mother, although her mother's reaction would have been worth seeing. But it wouldn't have happened. That was the point. They had been so very much in love. Had they been the exception to the rule?

Theo walked to one of the chairs in the corner and sat. She put his card on the bottom of the stack and stared at the name *Lord Sonden*. Nothing else was written on the card but, of course it was the calling card of Dabney Adams, her knight in shining armor for the evening. The poor man. What a mistake he made in choosing that particular veranda. He'd probably only wanted a breath a fresh air, as fresh as it got this time of year, and ended up saddled with her.

What did she know about him other than he was the most handsome man she had ever seen? And attentive and courteous and caring? Hiding behind his back was the safest she had felt in days, as silly as that was. She had experienced the irrational thought that if only she could cling to him, wrap her arms around his waist and refuse to let go, she would be safe.

Once she'd hopped over the railing like a wild country girl, and he'd followed, she had tried to excuse him. *That smile of his.* He'd made light of the situation and called it fun. He was a kind, wonderful, astonishingly handsome man. She extracted her fan and began to use it on her suddenly warm face.

"Are you alright?" A young woman asked her.

"Yes, thank you," Theo lied. "Just warm."

"It's stifling," the young woman agreed. "Why don't I get you some lemonade?"

"That's very kind of you."

"Not at all." The girl walked off. Theo noticed several of the others looking in her direction. Why? Was there something odd about how she looked? Besides red in the face? She turned her attention back to the cards as she flipped to Mr. Charles Pugh. At least, he had told her the truth about Hib's debt. She would definitely choose him over Sir Amos, she decided. They would be able to have an honest conversation. There would be friendship and laughter and camaraderie.

The young woman returned with a glass of lemonade for her. "Here you are."

"Thank you." Theo took a drink. "That helps."

The young woman sat in the chair beside her. "None of us know you," she said with an interested smile.

"Do you all know each other?" Theo asked. There were at least twelve or thirteen of them by now, perhaps more.

"Not well, but ... yes. We each know who the others are."

"I'm Theodora Martel."

"Of?"

Theodora blinked. "Pardon me?"

"Who is your father? Your family?"

It was asked gently enough that it was not as intrusive as it might have been. "My late father was Lord Chausterfield."

"I don't know him."

"No," Theo said, smoothing her skirt. She took another sip. "We are from Dover."

"That explains it. I'm Lady Julia Hamilton. My father is Lord Greendale."

She'd said it as if was supposed to mean something. "It's a pleasure to make your acquaintance."

"And yours. Who is your betrothed?"

Theo froze. She didn't want to say. "Do you know a Lord Sonden?" she asked haltingly.

Julia looked thoughtful. "It does sound familiar, but no."

A few others were wandering her way, and Theo needed to escape the inquiries she felt coming. "Is there a retiring room or privy we can use?" she asked quietly.

"There is a chamber pot behind the screen in the corner," Julia replied just as quietly, gesturing to it. "Or you can ask them to let you use another that's more private."

Theo nodded, smiled, and left Lady Julia to tell her friends what she'd learned. As if it was interesting. She fervently hoped that none of them knew who Sonden was. She had not meant to drag him into this mess. She went to the door and opened it, only to be warily surveyed by the three, count them, *three,* footmen guarding the door.

"May we help you, Miss?" one asked.

"Is there a retiring room I might use?"

"I'm afraid not. The announcements are to begin soon."

Theo took a breath and released it. The very walls reverberated with sounds of music, conversation and laughter. She was imprisoned here while the rest of the throng were having a gay old time. Could she beg or reason her way out? Could she pretend to be sick and then make a mad dash for it?

"It is time, girls," a lady called from the salon.

"You see," one of the footmen said. "It's time." He closed the door.

Rude! She turned back to the two ladies who had gathered everyone's attention.

"Miss Torrence. You are first."

"You will tell us what to do?" Miss Torrence fretted.

"Of course, dear. After you all are lined up. Lady Julia? Yes, there you are. You are second."

There was nervous giggling and chattering. They were all so happy. Everyone but her. She felt such dread she could barely breathe.

"Miss Margaret Partridge. Yes, there you go, dear. Miss Theodora Martel?"

Theo went forward. It felt as if she was joining the line to a mass execution.

"Miss Walsh, you shall be fifth."

What if she fainted? When it was her turn, what if she simply crumpled? She had never been a fainting sort of girl, but who knew that other than her? What was it Laurel had said? That she wasn't the weeping and wailing sort. Well, she felt like it now. Amidst all this giddy female anticipation.

Think!

Life with Charles Pugh. She tried to imagine sitting at the dinner table with him and talking over the events of the day. He wanted to marry her. He'd said he would be a good husband and she did not doubt that he would try. Did he make her feel breathless and weak kneed the way that Dab did? No. But at least he wanted to marry her. Dab was merely being gracious and noble, trying to buy her time to find a new path forward. It was not fair to put him in that position when he had simply chosen the wrong veranda that evening.

If she chose Charles Pugh, he would expect a commitment. A marriage. If she backed out after tonight, he might not forgive her. Cyrus would definitely not forgive her. He would be livid, and he would strike back somehow. How? He either had or was selling everything her parents had owned. Beyond that, what could he do?

The lady in charge clapped her hands. "If I may have your attention," she called. When it was quiet, she continued. "There will be a curtain blocking you from view until you are escorted up the steps and onto the stage. Before you step up, hand the card of your betrothed to the footman who will be escorting you. He will take it to the master of ceremonies once you are in position on stage. Does everyone understand?"

What was the most ideal moment for fainting?

"Your fiancé will join you on stage when his name is called and the two of you will bask in the moment, as well you should," she added with a smile. "Then the two of you will exit to the rear and then offstage. Others will be directing you."

"I'm so nervous," someone said behind her. It was followed by laughter of concurrence and murmurings of encouragement.

"After all are announced, there will be a dance solely for all of you. Alright? Any questions?"

There were not any. The doors to the ballroom were opened and the sound of music swelled. Theo realized she might not have to feign passing out. For once in her life, she felt shaky enough to do it. Or, at least, to fake it well. But would Cyrus step up and make the decision for her? She couldn't allow that to happen.

Chapter Nine

akely meandered by Cora Palmes, caught her eye, and discreetly gestured for her to follow. It took several moments for Cora to comply. She was clearly puzzled when she reached the secluded spot in the corridor where Lakely waited. "Did you wish to speak with me?"

"Yes." Cora was prettier than Lakely had realized. "Or rather my friend does."

"Who is your friend?"

"Dabney Adams."

Cora smiled. "Oh."

"He did not want to make a *show* of speaking to you, you see."

Cora gasped. "He's not going to … not tonight? I'm not prepared. I would have worn a different gown."

Cora was equally excited and alarmed, which made Lakely regretful. "No! No, it's not that."

Comprehension dawned on Cora's face. "Then what?"

Dab was coming toward them accompanied by Ada. Ada stopped. Dab kept coming until he reached them. "Thank you," he said to Lakely, excusing her. She nodded and went to join her sister. The pair of them stood together hoping to shield Dab and Cora from prying eyes. It wasn't necessary, because announcements were about to begin, and guests were ready and waiting.

Dab needed to tell Cora as quickly and painlessly as possible. "Something happened this evening," he said. "Something may yet happen, and I didn't … I do not want you caught unaware by it." Damn it, he was making a hash of it.

She looked concerned. "What's happened?"

"Earlier this evening, I went for a smoke, and I ended up encountering a lady," he began.

The brides-to-be were safely blocked from view of the audience. Some of them fidgeted nervously, others practically oozed eagerness.

Theo had two cards in hand. The card for Charles Pugh was in her right hand. The card of Lord Sonden was in her left. It made more sense to choose Mr. Pugh. It would please him, satisfy Hib, and disentangle Dab from further involvement. She was not likely to end up happy no matter how things went, so why not choose the person that created the least amount of damage?

Staring straight ahead, she shuffled the two cards. If only Dab had been one of the original choices, someone who actually desired marriage, her decision would be easy. But this was not fair to him.

Help me make the right decision, she prayed.

She stopped shuffling.

Whichever card is on top...

She looked down at the card in her hand. It was that of Charles Pugh. She sighed with resignation.

"You sent your card," Cora repeated in disbelief. "For her."

"Yes."

"So she could—" She could not even finish the statement.

He nodded, understanding what she meant. "My name could be called."

"And you'll go along with it?" she asked with vexation.

He suddenly saw the resemblance to her father. Cora was usually gracious, but she was used to getting her own way. "Yes."

"What are you thinking? It will be in the papers! All of them."

"I realize that."

"It will be a ...a humiliation for me. Do you understand that?"

"That is the last thing I want," he said earnestly. "But I never felt we were—"

"What? Well-matched? Am I not beautiful enough?"

"No! That's not it and it's not true. I was going to say we were not so far progressed enough to have discussed feelings."

"Discussed them," she scoffed. "Did you even have them for me?"

He didn't want to hurt her, but how was he to get around it?"

She took a step back. "You didn't," she realized with astonishment. "You don't."

"Cora, you are lovely and accomplished—"

"Please don't," she snapped. "Do you think I need or desire words of pity?"

"It is not pity."

She looked away. "Would you mind leaving me alone?"

He bowed his head to her and then walked away, feeling like a pile of steaming horse manure.

Dab walked past Ada and Lakely with a look of appeal they understood. Lakely went back to Miss Palmes. "Are you alright?" she asked gently.

Cora was watching Dab walk away. "I feel foolish."

"You should not," Lakely rejoined with a shake of her head.

Cora looked at Lakely. "My father told me that Mr. Adams' feelings did not run deep. Not for anyone or anything."

Lakely bit her tongue to keep from responding. The assertion was utterly untrue, but the girl was lashing out from the sting of rejection. Lakely understood that well enough. She had done the same not long ago.

"I am relieved to know it for myself," Cora added. "Even if his name is not called this evening, I am finished with him. I deserve better." Cora lifted her chin and walked back to a door of the ballroom, but she did not enter. Lakely went back to her sister and, together, they returned to the ballroom.

The dancing had ceased, and the crowd was ready for the next bit of entertainment. The main event. A group of gentlemen stood ready for their names to be called near the left side of the stage. Dab was in the middle of the audience. Being pinned in was making him even more anxious than he already was until Hugh stepped up beside him, purposely nudging his shoulder. Nigel was beside Hugh. Jonathan and JG closed in on Dab's other side. "I feel so protected," Dab jested.

"It's our intention to protect you," Hugh said. "Although I'm not sure it's you that will need protecting. Miss Martel, on the other hand ... if your name is called—"

"How about this," Dab said. "I'll protect her, and you protect me."

"What do you think will happen?" Jonathan asked Dab. "Will your name be called?"

"I have no idea," Dab admitted.

"I cannot wait to see her," JG said enthusiastically.

The others all gave him a look.

"What?" JG asked.

It was strange to stand there waiting. Dab felt as if a week had passed in the course of a few hours. What would Theo do? He was ridiculously nervous, but was it for her or for himself? He could not tell which it was.

"Ladies and gentlemen," the master of ceremonies called. The crowd quieted. "I stand center stage only for a moment, for tonight belongs to those lucky few who have found love," he said with a flourish, "or at least a lifetime commitment," he added to the amusement of most.

Dab was not among them.

"I tease, of course. This is, in truth, momentous. For what is more sacred than marriage? Tonight, we share in the joy of these solemn accords. So, without further ado." A string quartet began playing, and the master of ceremonies lifted his hand to the right side of the stage. "I am pleased to present Miss Catherine Torrence."

He stepped left as a handsome, light-haired footman escorted a lady in her mid-twenties onto the stage. The footman left her beaming in the middle of the stage and continued to the master of ceremonies to discreetly pass on a card.

"Daughter of Sir Roger and Lady Naomi Torrence," the master of ceremonies added. Already, Miss Torrence's intended was coming from the other side. "Miss Torrence is betrothed to Mr. Alexander Collinsworth."

There was a smattering of polite applause, and appreciative murmurs and comments about how fitting the pair looked together. He escorted her backstage, the front curtains parting elegantly for them. Already, the next lady appeared on the arm of another attractive footman.

"Presenting Lady Julia Hamilton." She was apparently well known enough to create a stir of interest. "Daughter of the Earl and Countess of Greendale. As was alluded to the most recent Society's Spectaculars, Lady Julia will wed the right honorable Mr. John William McTierny."

A few in the audience craned their necks to see the couple, but Dab's attention was on the next lady in line.

"Next, it is my honor to present Miss Margaret Partridge, newly betrothed to Sir Nathan Powell, baronet."

Mr. Powell tripped over his own two feet, but quickly recovered. It caused the couple a bit of embarrassment and there was some tittering in the audience, but Dab's full attention was on Theo, who had appeared on the arm of a footman. His breath caught as she found him in the crowd.

Hugh and Jonathan both glanced at him.

"Is that her?" JG whispered. "She is adorable!"

Dab could not tear his eyes from her. It was as if time had ground to a full stop. She looked apologetic. *Oh, God.* She was going to choose one of the others. She gave him a sad smile and looked away. She was going to choose one of the others. His heart hammered despite it being heavy with dread.

No. Don't do it. Don't do it, Theo.

"Presenting Miss Theodora Martel, daughter of the late and sister to the current Lord Chausterfield."

The card had already been passed on. Dab watched the footman deliver it. There would be nothing he could do once the name was read. Had she chosen another?

No. Please, no.

"Betrothed to … Lord Sonden."

Dab sighed with such great relief, he felt dizzy for a moment. He smiled and made his way toward the stage.

Theo was trembling. She had been for some time. She had not been able to stop herself from choosing Dab. She was sorry for dragging him further into her mess, and she had tried to convey as much when she spotted him, but then, when his name was called, he'd smiled the most magnificent smile.

There was commotion from the audience as Dab stepped onto the stage. Even the master of ceremonies seemed stunned. He said, "Lord Sonden who is … Mr. Dabney Adams."

Theo was confused by the reaction of shock and disbelief. People in the crowd were positively dazed to see him. One young woman had begun crying. Others seemed dismayed. Theo looked to Dab. He was almost to her. His gaze was steady, his expression confident. He offered his hand, and she took hold of it, but would her legs move? Would they even continue holding her up?

He pulled her hand through his arm and led her away. Behind them, everyone was talking at once. The curtains pulled open from the top in drapey scallops and closed behind them. The two of them kept walking. Even the couples who had gone before her gawked at Dab. Why? Who in the world was he?

The announced couples were supposed to gather backstage until the introductions were completed, but Dab kept going, and no one stopped them. The ladies in line were slack jawed to see him.

In the salon, alone for the moment, she turned to him. She wanted to understand who he was that had caused such a reaction, and she needed to apologize. To explain and to thank him and to promise that she would extricate herself from his life as soon as it was possible, but she was utterly stymied.

"I think it will be best if we duck out before the next segment," he ventured.

Before Hib got to her and attempted to throttle her. "I don't know if we can. I tried to leave earlier, and they wouldn't let me."

Just then a man popped in from the corridor. "Are we sneaking out?" he asked.

"Yes," Dab replied. He wrapped an arm around her hand and they started toward him.

There were four men in the hall. "These are my friends," Dab said.

"Hello, Theo," said a ginger-haired man with a smile.

Before she could return the greeting, Dab's friends had surrounded and hustled them onward. Outside, the thugs that caught her earlier, tried to intervene.

"I don't think so," one of Dab's friends said. "I box with Gentleman Jackson."

"We are armed," the thug warned.

The ginger haired man scoffed. "We are all armed," he retorted. "And I, myself, am a crack shot."

They all kept walking.

"Did you take a cab?" one of the friends asked Dab, who nodded.

"Then take our carriage," he offered.

"Theo! Dabney," a lady called. It was Mary who had rushed head of Bert, although he had practically broken into a jog.

Dab smiled. "Our new friends. Bert and Mary," he explained.

Mary was out of breath when she reached them. "That was the most exciting thing I have ever seen," she declared. "Now let us go quickly before your brother catches on that you've gone," she said to Theo.

As the Turner's carriage left with the older couple, Theo and Dab, his friends watched in amazement. Nigel turned to the others. "That was Dab, wasn't it?"

Jonathan slapped his leg. "That is what I have been saying!"

JG grinned. "That is what love can do, my friends. Sometimes it creeps up on a man, other times, it's a bloody thunderbolt." The others smirked and then burst into laughter. JG shrugged, unbothered. "It's true."

Hugh clapped his shoulder. "I will have to take your word for that."

"You've turned into such a philosopher, JG," Jonathan commented as they started back inside.

"Philosopher and wise man," JG said.

"Yes. That's what I meant to say. And who knew you were armed this evening?"

"Not to mention a crack shot," Nigel laughed.

Jonathan gave Hugh a wry look. "You do realize you're the odd man out now?"

Nigel chortled. "Come now. Let's not get ahead of ourselves. I saw what you saw, but Dab just met Theo."

Jonathan grunted. "Something like you and Alice the first time you met?"

Hugh nodded. "Or Jocelyn and JG at last year's Buckley's Ball."

"A bloody thunderbolt," JG practically sang.

~~~

Neither Sir Amos nor Charles Pugh had known which of their names would be called so they were both near the stage when the fiasco played out. Cyrus Martel stood behind them gaping in disbelief. He felt panic set in, especially as Sir Amos turned to him, red-faced with resentment and embarrassment.

Sir Amos stepped closer. "Your debt to me is now due," he said. He did not even wait for a response, he simply walked on.

"Cyrus?" his wife uttered.

She hadn't known about the debt. "Not now," he said under his breath.

Charles Pugh was also coming closer, but his reaction was markedly different than the man he'd seen as his competitor. Pugh seemed almost amused. "Looks as though she outsmarted you, Martel," he said when he reached him.

"I can get her back," Cyrus declared.

Pugh shrugged. "Pearce called in the debt, did he not? He said he would. Encouraged me to do the same if he won. He is no admirer of yours."

Cyrus's blood ran cold.

"He actually expected to win," Pugh said lightly. "Some men's vanity knows no bounds."

"Do you want her or not?"

Pugh thought about it and nodded. "More than ever, I think."

"I will get her back."

"I will give you three days. No, let's make it a bit longer. By Friday morning, I will either have your sister in hand, meaning in my safekeeping, or your debt to me is called in forthwith." He held Cyrus's gaze and then turned back to the stage where the master of ceremonies was trying to continue with the announcements. Unfortunately for him, Dabney Adam's appearance had set the place on its ear. "What a show," Pugh said. He was grinning as he left.

"What debts?" his irate wife hissed.

He glared at her. "Not now! I have to get to Theodora and try not to wring her neck until she's dead."

"Those are my diamonds she is wearing," Mildred reminded him.

"I will get them back," he bit out.

Chapter Ten

Theo felt as if she had been buffeted in a whirlwind and then abruptly released … but had not yet recovered her breath or her balance. She sat next to Dab and across from Mary and Bert in the carriage, all of them swaying to and fro, and he was still holding her hand. Of course, her grip was tight enough that perhaps he had not been able to release it.

What had happened back there? She had chosen him out of sheer selfishness, despite what it did to his life and reputation, and then he'd seemed pleased by it. His gallantry far surpassed anything she could have expected. She looked at him. He smiled a tender smile at her and squeezed her hand.

"I should get out soon," he said. "I'll catch a cab and go see Maeve."

Theo nodded. She needed to snap out of this stupor and think.

"Do you want out now?" Bert asked him.

"Please," Dab said.

Bert rapped on the roof of the carriage which slowed and pulled over.

"May I call on you tomorrow?" Dab asked, addressing it to Mary.

"Of course, you may," Mary replied. "You must!" She opened her reticule and pulled out a card. "The address is on there. We'll be expecting you."

Dab looked at Theo. "I'll explain everything to Maeve," he said softly. "Don't worry."

She nodded. Did she even possess the strength to use her voice any longer?

"Are you alright?" he asked.

"Yes," she replied breathily. "I think so." She glanced at Bert and Mary. "I've never escaped before. It's rather overwhelming."

His smile broadened. "I'll see you tomorrow then."

She nodded. There was a moment's hesitation where she thought he might lean in and kiss her, but she was being utterly foolish. He got out of the carriage, and they drove on.

"Are you really alright?" Mary asked her worriedly.

Tears rushed to Theo's eyes. "What was that back there? That response when people saw it was him."

"It came as a surprise," Mary replied soothingly. "People were surprised. That's all." She paused. "Dab is well known because of his handsome face. The gossip columns have dubbed him Adonis."

Theo drew back. Adonis!

Bert gave Theo an empathetic smile. "I don't think they asked his permission first," he offered. "They write what they write to entertain and sell papers. Although why people find it entertaining, I could not say." He gave his wife a cynical glance.

"I do not deny reading it," she declared. "Have I ever denied it? I read it and enjoy it. I do not take it seriously."

"Pshaw! I've seen you mad as a hornet about something written about someone you don't even know."

"Well, yes. When something is cruel."

"She's written letters to the paper," Bert said to Theo.

"If one feels strongly, one should make it known," Mary stated.

He looked at her. "I feel strongly … about you." He finished it with a grin.

Mary giggled like a girl. "I feel strongly about you, but I don't feel a need to tell the papers about it."

"I think it might make a worthy story," he returned.

Bless them, Theo thought, as she dabbed at her eyes with the backs of her gloved fingertips. They had distracted her with their love and affection. They were fifty something years old and they still adored one another. As her parents had. How astonishing it was that she had not known them before this evening and now they felt like family.

Mary leaned forward to pat her leg. "All will be well. Never you worry. I feel it in my bones."

~~~

It was Maeve who opened the door when Dab rang the bell. Theo had not described her and yet Dab knew it was her.

"May I help you?" the lady asked tersely. Understandably. It was late.

"Theo sent me," he said.

Alarmed, she leaned out and looked around. "Where is she?"

"She is not here, but she is safe. She's with friends."

She gave him a hard look. "What friends?"

"New friends. May I come in for a moment?"

"I do not know you," she objected.

"Nor did Theo know me before tonight and yet it would seem... we are betrothed."

Maeve's jaw dropped. She remembered herself, closed it and stepped back. "You'd best come in and explain, sir."

He stepped into the modest townhome as Maeve closed the door behind him. "My name is Dabney Adams."

"Not one of the chosen few," she stated.

"Excuse me?"

"You were not one of the men selected by Cyrus, her cursed half-brother, for her to choose from."

"Ah. No. No, I was not."

"Then how—"

He held up his hand to halt her because it was possible Cyrus would show up any minute with his men, and it would make things worse for her if he was still there. "Theo panicked. She left the ballroom and eventually made her way onto a veranda I happened to be on. Cyrus was after her, so I quickly hid her. When the coast was clear, she explained the situation."

"Go on."

"We found a way for me to be announced as her betrothed, and then we hurriedly left the ball. She went home with our other friends who had helped, and I came here to explain things to you. She couldn't leave you worrying been waiting."

"Cyrus will be livid," Maeve stated.

"I imagine he is livid," Dab agreed. "Which is why she must stay hidden until the next part of the plan."

"Which is?"

"We haven't actually figured out the next part of the plan yet."

Maeve studied him a moment. "Dabney Adams, you say. And you did this out of the goodness of your heart?" she asked suspiciously.

"I assure you, I have no ulterior motives. I wanted to help her and so I did. It's really as simple as that." He retrieved Mary's calling card and offered it. He'd memorized the address. "This is where Theo is staying, but Cyrus cannot know, of course."

Maeve snapped it up. "Thank you."

"I should go. He may show up here tonight."

"I am quite certain of it."

"Will you be alright?"

She barked a laugh. "I will be fine."

He inclined his head to her and started to leave. "Goodnight, then."

"Thank you," she said again with more warmth than before. He turned back as she lifted her chin. "For telling me ... and for what you did."

He nodded.

"That girl is everything to us. Her mother was and she and her sisters are. Oh, but Theo ... is so special. You cannot possibly know. Nor could you know the torment she's been through these last many months."

He lingered because of a yearning to know. Somehow, he knew how unique and special she was. "I know she lost both parents."

Maeve nodded. "Yes. It's been a year now since her father's passing. He was older than her mother. He had come here for medical examinations, which did not turn out well, so we were given to understood he had a limited amount of time. It was his heart."

Dab nodded. Theo had said as much.

"Nothing could have prepared anyone for what happened to Scarlett and the girls on that bitter April day."

"Theo only said it was an accident."

"In a freezing rain," Maeve said hauntedly. "It was foolish to have left. Scarlett usually had better sense, but she would not be kept away from her Robert." She smiled sadly. "I've never known two people as in love as they were. At least, that is one good thing. They are together again. And little Rose with them."

He drew back.

Maeve saw his stunned reaction. "She didn't tell you?"

"No."

"Well, I will tell you as succinctly as I can, if you want to know."

"I do. Please."

She considered where to start. "Scarlett, Rose, Theo, and Greta, who was nineteen, she is twenty now, left for the city in a hired coach. There was only one family carriage, you see, and Robert had taken it to the city for the tests I mentioned." She paused. "On a narrow road above a cliff, something went terribly wrong." She paused again before adding, "The coach went over."

He released a breath he hadn't realized he'd been holding.

"Theo and Greta managed to get out before it went over, but Theo landed on the edge of the road. It was slippery, as you can probably imagine, and she couldn't keep a grip. She fell to a rocky outcrop below, which stopped her fall, Thank God, but her head hit hard. We all thought she would die. She woke days later … completely blind."

"Blind?"

She nodded before continuing. "Can you imagine what that was like for her? They were already to be the darkest days she'd ever known … metaphorically, but then there was the physical darkness, as well." She sighed, thinking back on it. "Her sight returned slowly, her health improved, but her spirit has never recovered in full. I have seen glimpses of it. Of course, I have hope. I will always have hope and faith in her. And now more than ever, thanks to you."

He thought about it all. "How old was Rose?"

"Five. Rose was her mother's shadow. I imagine she still is."

He felt a lump in his throat. "Thank you for telling me."

"Theo is the bright light of our lives. She deserves the freedom and the opportunity to shine. I am so grateful for the part you played in that."

He nodded. "I was glad to." He wished he could stay and hear more but this wasn't the time. "I should go."

"Goodnight, Mr. Adams."

"Goodnight."

Dab's mind was full of the story as he returned to his cab. He looked for another carriage approaching. He didn't see one and yet he could sense Cyrus Martel closing in. He had seen the arrogance and the determination in the man's face.

Damn him.

~~~

The walls of the bedroom Theo had been given were papered, a cranberry background with designs of golden fans and ivory scrolls. She walked around the room, wearing a too-large cotton nightgown she'd been lent, lost in thought about the newspaper articles she'd read.

Mary had given her copies of different papers and magazines, all of which had articles about individuals of *the ton*. Technically speaking, she was a member of that group, although she had never felt like it. She had no idea who the articles referred to. The subjects were Lady S. or Lord P. or Sir C. or aliases such as Golden Star or Adonis.

One thing was certain. Dab fascinated them. Otherwise, why write about who he had spent time with at this ball or danced with at that soiree? At least, she understood the audience's reaction tonight. He'd achieved fame. If most people read the papers, they probably thought they knew all about him. What could not be explained was the man himself. Why had he done it when he had every choice of available ladies open to him?

She walked over to the vanity table and sat with a sigh. No wonder they had all been so shocked. Plain Theo with Adonis, a mortal so beauteous, goddesses fought over him. What had she burdened him with? And what would the gossip pages report tomorrow about what had taken place tonight?

~~~

Dab was surprised to see light from beneath his mother's bedroom door. He'd been about to go into his own room, but he walked that way, pausing in the doorway of his father's room. It was empty and moonlit. The furniture had been sold. The walls were now painted a deep blue gray. Sheer white curtains hung in windows, fluttering in the night's breeze.

Dab no longer sensed his father here, so perhaps his mother had been right about changing the room out entirely. He walked on and tapped lightly on her door.

"Yes?" she called.

He opened the door. She was stretched out in a chaise lounge with a glass in hand and an open book on her lap. "You're up late," he commented.

"Sleep has begun eluding me since your father left."

Since your father left seemed a strange description. As if he'd left voluntarily.

"How was the ball?"

He leaned against the door jamb. "It started out quite usually, I suppose, although it felt odd to be out. At first, it felt … I felt hollow, if that makes any sense."

She nodded and murmured her understanding.

"But it turned into something altogether different."

"Really? Come in and tell me. I'm intrigued."

He walked further in. He had not been inside her room in many years. It was pleasant and feminine, done in shades of white and cream. Her hair was loose, and she wore a satin wrapper of indigo. There were more strands of gray in her hair than he'd realized.

"Would you care for some port?" she asked. A decanter of it was on the table beside her on a mirrored tray that held an empty glass.

"That sounds good. Thank you." He sat in the chair next to hers and accepted the delicate cordial glass she offered. Port wasn't a particular favorite of his, but this was a good one, rich and not overly sweet.

"So, it began normally," she said with an interested gleam in her eye. "Hundreds of guests, music, dancing."

He nodded. "It was quite a crowd. Six hundred, I was told. There was a lady in attendance, Miss Cora Palmes. I was trying to avoid her. Or, rather, I wanted it to appear that I did not see her. I didn't want to appear to rebuff her, but I also didn't want to fuel the speculation. Some of the papers have paired us off as an item."

She nodded. "I've read," she admitted.

He grinned and leaned back. "Someone asked me tonight how my parents feel when they read something written about me."

"And what did you say?"

"I said my father had very recently passed, but that he saw the humor in it."

She smiled wistfully. "For me, it's different at different times, depending on what was written. For the most part, it doesn't really seem like you. Perhaps there is some truth behind the things that are written, but it always strikes me as more of a ... puppet show."

He nodded. "I wish they cared that it impacted people," he said. "Not me, so much, but others. Ladies. Cora, for example." He took another drink. "I was actually summoned before her father not long ago to determine my interest in her."

"Which does not appear to be overly much," his mother mused. "She's an heiress, I read."

"She is. I even wondered about the prudence of marrying her."

She flinched. "Prudence?"

"Yes. In the last year, I have seen most of my friends fall head over heels in love. I've wished I could feel anything remotely like it."

"Oh, Dab. You will!"

"I've never thought so. I had decided wasn't capable of falling in love. So why not marry into wealth and get on with it? Have a family and no financial worries. I've always known I would love a child."

She looked crushed by his admission. "You will," she said thickly. "You will love them with a ferocity and depth you did not know you possessed."

There was so much they still had to talk about. So much that had to be aired out between them. Was this the time? She looked away and reached into her pocket for a handkerchief, then dabbed at her eyes and nose. He looked down at the glass in his hands. "My friends were giving me what for tonight," he said in a lighter tone. "It's what we do."

She smiled.

"So, I walked away to have a smoke. Or so I said. I went to one of the verandas on the side of the house. Most were occupied, but one only had a single occupant, a gentleman on it, puffing on a cigar. He struck me as amiable, and he was. We chatted, and then his wife joined us. She was as much of a character as he was. I mean that in a good way. They are salt of the earth. Bert and Mary Turner."

She shifted toward him, pulling up her legs.

"Bert started back inside to get more drinks, but a young lady nearly collided with him. She was distressed, as though she was running from someone … and she was. Her half-brother, trying to force her into a marriage she doesn't want." He paused. "I hid her from the half-brother. His name is Cyrus Martel. Lord Chausterfield."

"And her name?"

"Theo." He smiled. "Miss Theodora Martel from Dover. They call her Theo."

"What was she like?"

"She is pretty with hair of light brown and gold. Eyes of amber. Pretty. Did I already say that? She struck me as delicate but … later I learned what she's been through. She is anything but delicate. Or rather she's delicate but also resilient and strong and brave."

Charlotte released a small huff of astonishment and delight. "So, meeting this lady. That's what was unusual?"

"There is more. When her brother had walked on, after we successfully hid her, she explained her situation, that he had given her two choices for a husband. Tonight was the Betrothal Ball."

She nodded.

"He wanted it announced. In fact, it had been arranged. The reason he had been searching for her was to get her decision as to which of the men it would be. All she wanted to do was escape."

"I understand," she rejoined. "If it was being forced on her."

"It was and we did understand. The problem was that she had nowhere to go. Her parents are gone, both in the last year or so."

"Oh, dear."

"Her elder sisters have offered to take her in, but they don't really have the means. So, Mary declared that Theo would stay with them. She wouldn't take no for an answer."

Charlotte smiled. "I like Mary, already."

He nodded. "You will. And Bert. At that point, once Theo had agreed, the choice was either to walk out of the house and chance being seen or go over the railing of the veranda and sneak around the house to the Turner's carriage. I offered to lift her over." He grinned and nearly laughed. "She hopped over the fence in her beautiful pale blue gown."

Charlotte laughed. "Oh, my!"

"Naturally, I followed."

"Naturally," she agreed as she poured them each more port, although her glass wasn't empty.

"Midway around the house, she tried to excuse me from further assistance. She feared she'd wasted enough of my time. I told her that I hadn't had as much fun at any ball that I remembered. Then I took the lead and had her wait at the edge of the house while I went to find the carriage. Bert had gone ahead to arrange things with their driver, but by the time I found him and started back to get Theo, two men had grabbed her and were forcing her back into the house."

Charlotte's eyes were round, her jaw lax. "What men?"

"Men her brother obviously hired."

"How strange."

He nodded. "Whatever Chausterfield has on the line must be significant. To go to that much planning and expense? He must have suspected she would try to get away."

"What did you do?"

"I didn't know what to do. I returned to the ball, found my friends, and told them what was going on. I learned all the ladies to be announced were being kept in the salon next door to the ballroom, but the doors were guarded."

"This is all sounding very strong-armed," she remarked.

"I would venture that every lady wanted to be there, except for Theo. But I could not even get a message to her, so Lakely, Nigel's sister, you met them all after the funeral—"

She nodded.

"She went in and spoke to Theo."

"And said what?"

"She offered Theo my card."

Charlotte cocked her head in confusion.

"Theo had been trapped, you see. It seemed she only had two choices to make. I wanted to offer a third."

"Yourself," Charlotte said quietly.

"Well, yes. We had discussed her escaping and I had seen the light in her eyes when she thought it was a real possibility."

"But, darling, running away and hiding is one thing. Offering yourself as a replacement..."

"I thought it still might amount to the same thing. By then, I'd learned that the announcements would be highly orchestrated. First, the lady to be announced was escorted up on stage. She handed the card of her betrothed to an escort who gave it to the master of ceremonies who announced it."

She nodded.

"Then the fiancé stepped up and together they walked off stage. All the while music is playing, and the crowd is craning their necks to see them. Reporters jotting down notes."

"What did she do? What did she say?"

"Lakely said she was touched and surprised to receive the card, but she didn't say what she would do. So, I stood helplessly in the crowd and waited." He paused. "I could simply blurt out what happened, but I feel you ought to be tortured a bit as I was."

She grinned. "Then by all means, torture away."

"They announced the first lady and then her betrothed, and then the second and third. Theo was fourth."

Charlotte swung her legs around and sat facing him.

"She looked so vulnerable, Mother. She saw me and gave me this sad smile. My heart ... it dropped. I was so sure she was going to choose one of the others." He paused, but his mother was waiting breathlessly for him to continue. "Then my name was called."

She gasped.

"It was a shock to the crowd, too. I made my way up there, got her and we left. Snuck out, to be more precise, surrounded by Nigel and Hugh and Jonathan and JG. Martel's hired thugs tried to stop us, but they were outnumbered." He chuckled. "Jonathan telling them he boxes with Gentleman Jackson. JG saying we were all armed and he was a crack shot. Nigel trying to loan me their carriage."

"Dabney, are you saying—" She let the question trail off into silence.

"It was announced that we are betrothed."

"Ahh—"

"I don't know what's going to happen next. Right now, she's with Mary and Bert, safe for the moment. Perhaps she'll want to return to Dover, or she might choose to stay with one of her sisters. Tonight may have been nothing more than a temporary escape. I don't know. I'll see her again tomorrow and learn what she's thinking."

"I see. Her brother must be furious."

He nodded. "Without question."

"Oh, darling. I have no idea what will be in tomorrow's papers, but I am so proud of you." She reached out and took hold of his hand.

The words touched him.

"You saw a lady in need, one who was being wronged, and you stepped up and helped. Thank you for telling me."

"I was glad to share it. It would have come as quite the shock to read about it in the papers, had I not."

"Yes," she agreed. "It would have."

"Tomorrow you and I should discuss everything else," he said. "Air it out once and for all."

Her smile vanished, but she nodded.

He rose and bent to kiss her cheek. "Goodnight."

Chapter Eleven

*D*ab readied himself the next morning, had breakfast and decided to walk awhile. It was not even ten o'clock in the morning, too early for visiting, but Mary and Bert would not stand on formality.

He had slept decently but awakened feeling anxious. More than anxious, agitated. He felt a pressing need to get to Theo. He'd reached the front door when his mother called to him as she came down the stairs. She was still in her nightclothes and had a newspaper in hand.

"It's one of many, I'm sure," she said handing it over. It was folded back to the society page.

"Is it cruel to her?" he asked apprehensively.

"No, it's not. Nor to you." She reached out to smooth his lapel.

"I'll see you at dinner," he said before leaving with the paper in hand. He would walk off some of his nervous energy and then get a cab and read the column. He wanted to know what had been said about her.

He'd made it a block and a half before curiosity got the better of him and he stopped and scanned it. He saw his name and backed up to the beginning of the paragraph.

Thus far, the event had been mildly interesting, but far short of entertaining. The fourth name called, that of Miss Theodora Martel, a lady no one had ever heard of, changed things dramatically. She was pretty, in a wide-eyed, fresh-faced way. She struck this writer as a country girl

wearing her first fine gown and
jewelry, but one who would have
been forgotten by the end of the next
dance had the name of her betrothed,
Lord Sonden, not have shocked as it
did. For Lord Sonden is none other
than Dabney Adams. *Adonis!*

How the spectators gasped and
gawked. It had to be a ruse, some
swore. There were sighs and tears
from crestfallen hopefuls. By this
point, Miss Martel seemed as stunned
as anyone. Lord Sonden, however,
appeared supremely confident. He
went to her, held out his hand, and
off they went, leaving a staggered
audience.

The poor master of ceremonies
could not move on with the program
for the excitement and rampant
conjecture that erupted. Who was
she? Was the engagement real or a
stunt arranged by the hosts to
astound and amuse? Many still
wonder.

Dab folded the paper and walked on. He offered it to the next
man he passed, who accepted it with his thanks. Dab strode
onward with a scowl on his face. Fresh-faced country way, indeed.
"Wouldn't know quality and beauty if it bit your behind," he
muttered.

The Turner's home on Denbigh Street was in an upscale,
working-class neighborhood. A middle-aged maid let Dab in and
he was shown into the drawing room where Theo quickly joined

him wearing a simple day gown of yellow and gray. It had to be her own; it fit so well.

Her hands were clutched in front of her. "Hello," she said nervously. "Mary and Bert went to church."

"Oh. Yes, of course. Is it alright if I'm here? I could come back later."

"No! Please stay. It's fine. Would you care to sit?"

"Yes, but ... is there a garden we could walk or sit in?"

"There is a small garden." She turned, obviously self-conscious, and led the way to it.

The sides of the back yard were walled, and vines had enmeshed themselves in the brick as well as on the barks of large trees that provided dense shade. She led the way to three short benches set in a triangle formation, and they sat, facing one another.

"How are you?" he asked.

"I am of two minds," she began hesitantly. "I am glad for myself. And grateful. But I am sorry for the predicament you now find yourself in."

"I am not in a predicament," he stated. She looked away, blushing. "I'm not," he reiterated.

She looked back at him. "I read the paper this morning."

"What did it say that's bothered you?"

"How shocked everyone was. And that a few were devastated."

He shook his head. "They exaggerate."

"People were shocked. I saw it. That is no exaggeration. A Miss Palmes was mentioned as was Miss Hart and Lady Eleanor."

His smile had vanished. "I never entered into any understanding with them or with anyone else. Spoken or implied." He paused. "Before last night, that is."

"You mustn't think I will hold you to anything! You did a valiant thing, which I will always be grateful for."

He had not envisioned the conversation going like this. "I saw Maeve," he said, purposedly changing the subject.

"I know. Thank you for that. She brought some things this morning. It must have been at the crack of dawn. There was a letter in it ... explaining."

"Did Cyrus pay her a visit after I left?"

She nodded. "He did, demanding to know where I was. She, in turn, demanded to know exactly what had happened and what he had done with me."

"Good."

"He had those men with him. They pushed in and searched the house high and low."

He frowned at the thought. "No one was hurt, though?"

"No. But before he left, Cyrus gloated that I only *thought* I had outsmarted him, but he always keeps an ace up his sleeve."

"He's blustering."

"I hope so."

"I must say Maeve is quite something."

She smiled. "Yes, she is. I've known her my entire life. She was in our household before I was."

"She told me about the accident," he volunteered reluctantly.

Theo studied him a moment.

"I am so sorry for what you've been through," he added.

She looked away with a soft sigh. "Most of us have known sorrow, even tragedy." She looked at him again. "I had a large dose of it, but I also had a joyful life with parents who adored one another and us. And we adored them. Not everyone is as fortunate as that."

"That is very true."

"What of your life, Lord Sonden? The papers hint that you may be unknowable."

His title on her lips felt wrong. "Is that how I strike you?"

"No. Not at all. But nor do I know you well."

"I am not unknowable, Theo. My friends know me, and I know them."

"You have very good friends. I saw that."

"Yes, I do. I have held a part of my life back from them," he admitted. "From everyone. Perhaps it shaped me more than I realized."

"Why have you held back part of your life from them?"

He considered how to answer and decided on the truth. "It's difficult to explain, but I suppose the long and short of it is that I was ashamed of it." He stood and walked over to a fragrant evergreen tree pondering whether he should have said *I am ashamed of it.*

She also rose and meandered closer. She bent to pick a daisy before turning back to him. "I am sorry it has taken such a toll on you, whatever it is."

He was relieved that she wasn't asking him to reveal it. He hoped that he might be able to one day, but not before he'd spoken to his mother about it. That had to be first.

"I'm going to fix up the garden for them," she said. "Mary does not enjoy gardening."

He could tell it wasn't well tended. "What does she enjoy?"

"People. Talking. Helping. Her husband."

He grinned. As she twirled the daisy in her hand, he realized she was the most beautiful thing he had ever seen. "I want you to know me," he said. "And I want to know you."

Her eyes widened. "I want that, as well."

He stepped closer. "I don't want to talk of sorrows. Let's begin with something happier. We'll work our way to the rest of it in time." He offered his arm, and she slipped her hand through. He didn't care that there wasn't far to stroll. He could have stood with her like that and been content.

"It's just that I don't want you to feel ... stuck," she fretted.

He shook his head. "I don't. And there will be no more of that, if you please. And no more Lord Sonden, either. It's too formal for us." He grinned wickedly. "We are engaged, after all."

She blushed. "Indeed. After knowing one another for all of ... fifteen minutes?"

He chuckled. "We are impetuous, are we not? So tell me what you enjoy," he said as they started to stroll.

.

Chapter Twelve

*I*t was past four in the afternoon when Dab returned home. It had been such a good day. He went upstairs and into the office, a paneled room with green walls and a window overlooking the street. He sat and placed his hands on the mahogany desk. The last time he sat there had been as a child playing grown up.

He took a deep breath and went through drawers inspecting each item lovingly. A magnifying glass. A long-stemmed pipe. A tin of tobacco. A ruler. Sharpened pencils and a pearl handled knife. His father's things. Only now they were his things. The baronage was his and it was time to take responsibility.

He pulled out a ledger and got to work. His father's writing was neat and precise, and the breakdown was logical. Dab quickly grasped the household expenses, the servants' salaries, even the cost of food and drink and coal. His parents had certainly not lived lavishly. Their total living expenses came to some thirty-five hundred pounds a year.

As for rendering payments for the household accounts, Fanning took care of some of it and the housekeeper, or rather former housekeeper, Mrs. Daniels, had paid the rest. What happened to Daniels? At present, only Fanning, the cook, a lady named Mrs. Foote, and two maids were employed. He did not even know the maids' names.

He leaned back in the chair. It felt as if he had just awakened from the world's longest sleep-walk, but he was wide awake now and biting at the bit. He pulled out some paper and went back to the ledger to begin tallying.

When a knock on the door startled him, he looked up to see his mother, and he realized the light had changed. He'd been engrossed for more than an hour.

"You seem hard at work," she commented.

"I'm getting my head around our finances."

"How was your day?"

"It was fabulous."

She studied him a moment. "Was it?"

He smiled. "Yes. I am not being sarcastic. Mary and Bert were at church when I arrived, so Theo and I spent time in the garden talking."

"How's she feeling after the events of last night?"

"She said she was glad and relieved for herself but she felt guilty for my part in it."

She nodded in understanding.

"An article she read mentioned the *devastation*, quote unquote, of certain ladies whom they then had the audacity to name. I told her it was all exaggeration. I've had no understanding with any lady ... until last night."

Charlotte cocked her head.

"She said she would never hold me to that," he added quickly. "In her eyes, I rescued her for the evening, but I owed her nothing further ... and I had her eternal gratitude."

Charlotte smiled. "I like this girl," she said.

"You will love her. I realize this will probably be shocking, which is what I seem to be doing lately, but I intend to make her your daughter-in-law."

Her smile vanished. "Dabney, you have been caught up in something momentous but please do not rush into any decision that will affect the rest of your life. Both of your lives."

"I won't," he assured her. "I have not declared anything. Nor will I for some time. I was just telling you."

"Oh. Well ... just please take your time. Clearly, she's turned your head, but marriage is a lifetime commitment."

"I know it is. I see now how wrong I was to even consider the idea of marrying Cora." His mother still looked disturbed. "I have a few questions about the finances," he said. "Will you sit a moment?"

"Of course." She moved to the chair in front of his desk and sat gracefully.

"What happened to Daniels?" he asked.

"She left over a year ago. An illness in her family required her attention."

"And you've done without a housekeeper since."

"Yes."

"You don't need one?"

She gave a light shrug. "We learned to manage without."

"Because of the expense," he guessed.

"Yes. A good housekeeper costs at least twenty-five pounds a year. We learned to make do without a great deal of inconvenience."

"I see," he murmured. "What are the maids' names?"

The question seemed to surprise her. "The one with the birthmark on her face is Yolanda. The other is Hazel. They do their work efficiently and quietly."

Which did not excuse him from not knowing their names and acknowledging them. "It looks to me like we only have eighteen thousand pounds in funds. Does that sound correct?"

She glanced down at her hands, embarrassed. "It's not that much."

"I was including the stipend that's been set aside for me and never touched."

She flushed. "I see. Then, yes. That sounds correct."

He made a face. "I don't suppose we'll be throwing any grand parties soon."

"No."

"And let us hope the roof does not begin leaking. I am teasing, of course."

She grinned and shrugged.

"Whatever became of Standon Cottage? Was it sold?"

"No. There is a man, Frederick Cross, who keeps watch and does whatever maintenance is needed to keep it intact. That's really all we've been able to do."

He nodded. "I saw the monthly payments to Cross. I wondered what they were. When was the last time you were there?"

"Oh, gracious. Years. In fact, you were with us. You must have been nine or ten."

He leaned back. He hadn't thought about the place in years.

"Your father has been there since, but not in four or five years, at least. It's not livable. I'm certain it would require far more care than it's received not to mention refurbishing."

"Given the finances, why wasn't it sold? I remember there is acreage with it."

She nodded. "Two hundred acres. It wasn't sold because we felt it was yours. Your legacy."

"It bears looking into. It's in Hertfordshire, isn't it?"

"Yes. Seven miles outside of Hertford. It's only a half-day's ride from here. I can write out the directions if you want to go see it."

"I do."

"If that's all for now, I should get ready for dinner."

"I'll see you down there."

She hesitated. "And then we can talk about—"

He nodded and watched as she rose and left.

Mother and son sat at opposite ends of the table. Both picked at their food. Neither had any appetite. "How do we begin?" she finally asked, pushing her plate back.

"I don't know," Dab admitted. "It's been packed away and held in for so long, I don't know."

"You were able to forgive your father," she ventured carefully.

"Yes."

It was silent a few moments before she said, "What did you forgive him for?"

He cocked his head. "You know very well what for."

"I'm asking what precisely I need to be forgiven for in your view. I know where my fault lies in my own mind and heart. I am wondering what you think."

He hated this subject. He frowned as he reached for his wine. "I feel … I've always felt that you should have known."

She blinked, surprised by the response. "Known?"

He set the wine back down. He didn't want it. His stomach was knotted. "Yes. You should have known what she was all about. Known that—" He faltered. "I don't even know how to express it."

"Known that she encouraged you," she said haltingly.

He could not believe his ears. "Encouraged me?" he exclaimed, causing her to jump. "God almighty! Encouraged me? Was that what she said when she *confessed*?"

She was too stunned and taken aback to reply. Tears filled her eyes.

He huffed as he looked away.

"Dab," she said gently. "What is it?"

He glared at her. "What do you think happened? After all this time. After all these years, what is it you think happened?"

She made a breathy utterance, unable to form words.

He rose, came closer, sitting in the chair next to her. "Tell me," he added in a more restrained tone.

She placed her folded hands on the table and stared at them. "Florence was a very beautiful woman."

He chewed on his tongue.

"Younger than your uncle. Younger than me. You were a boy. You got confused. She was flirtatious."

He felt a sinking pit of despair open up deep within. It felt enormous, bigger than he was. "I was a child," he said softly.

She looked at him. Her dark eyes looked so like his own. "Yes. You were a child. You were our child. I think you must have … touched her by accident the first time. And perhaps you experienced a certain … pleasurable feeling from it."

"Stop," he ordered. She looked confused and even helpless, but this was all wrong. "You wrote me," he said in a low voice. "You and Father wrote, both saying that she *confessed*. I was thirteen at the time and it did nothing but make me furious. Because *she* confessed and so you believed me, but it was too late as far as I was concerned. Because you should have known. You should have known me and you should have known her and you should have known what was happening. That's what my thinking was then and … it has been my thinking all this time."

Her jaw had gone lax.

"What exactly did she *confess*?"

"Th-that she had encouraged you. Without meaning to," she stammered.

He slammed his hand on the table, nearly upsetting her glass of wine. "She seduced me. She touched me … in ways I knew were wrong, but she was the adult."

His mother sat back. She looked pale and unsteady.

"Looking back on it, I see that she groomed me. Little by little from a very young age."

Tears had begun to stream down her face, and she made no attempt to staunch them.

"Good God! You didn't know, did you?"

She shook her head and gasped for air. She tried to speak, but only a choked sound came out. "I knew s-something—"

He sighed and laid his hand on her arm. "Stop. Breathe. You will make yourself sick."

It was too late. She was past the point of no return. She convulsed with sobs. When she shook her head, held up her hands and left the room, he did not try to stop her. He was furious with himself. All the years of silence and distance to punish them had played right into Florence's tale, one in which he was the deviant and she had merely and accidentally encouraged him.

From the day his uncle had brought him home railing about having found them in a compromising situation, he should have said something. He should have shouted that *she* was the monster. He should have said it and he should have kept on saying it. But he hadn't been certain of it or of anything. She had made him complicit, always calling him her special boy and swearing him to secrecy. No one would understand them, she'd declared. No one understood how lonely she was or how very special he was to her. She had made him feel extraordinary and chosen in the moment, and then dirty and wrong afterward. He had been eleven when they were caught and the secret blew up in their faces.

Chapter Thirteen

D ab left his room the next morning and saw one of the maids backing out of his mother's room with an empty tray in hand. Hazel. "Good morning," he said to her after she closed the door.

She stopped, surprised by the greeting, and curtsied. "Good morning, sir. My lord," she stammered.

He took a few steps closer. "How is my mother?"

She seemed reluctant to answer." I don't believe she had the best night."

He nodded." Thank you, Hazel." She blushed and quickly walked on clutching the tray to her chest. He tapped lightly on his mother's door and then cracked it open. "Mother?"

"Come in," she said.

He opened the door and stepped inside. She was sitting in bed with an untouched tray table in front of her. He could tell it had been a sleepless night for her. "Did you sleep at all?"

"A little. I know because of the nightmare I had."

He closed the door and came closer. "I feel I should apologize."

She looked incredulous. "For what? For telling the truth? I am the one who should apologize. Although that's worthless now, isn't it?"

He sighed and motioned to the bedside chair. "May I?"

"Of course."

He sat before speaking. "I see now how wrong I was in the way I handled what happened. I made a bad situation immeasurably worse."

She cringed. "You were a boy!"

He nodded slowly. "Who knew the truth about something and did not say what it was. And as I grew up, I held on to my anger and silence like it was a shield... and a sword."

She sighed.

"You and I are both as sorry as can be," he said quietly. "It is time we stopped apologizing. Stop revisiting and dissecting the mistakes of the past. I see how wrong I was, and I hope you will forgive me for it. And you have apologized over and over again."

"But not for the right thing," she agonized.

"Mamma," he said quietly with a shake of his head.

"What kind of a mother doesn't know her child is being hurt? I *knew* something was different. That you were … changing. More secretive. More closed off, somehow. I thought it was just what boys went through. I didn't know!"

"I know," he replied tenderly. "Can we put it behind us?"

"I so want to, my love. But what that woman has gotten away with," she uttered with a shake of her head. "We have to face her and tell your uncle."

Perhaps she was right. Then it could truly be left behind. "Alright."

"Today," she said.

"Agreed. When is the last time one of the carriages was used?"

"A while. A year, I suppose," she replied with a shrug.

"I'll take a look at them and rent a horse." He stood. "Eat something," he urged.

"I will."

He bent and kissed her cheek. "We will get through this."

She gave him a smile. "We will, won't we?"

He nodded. "And be better and stronger for it."

Dab wrote a note to Theo explaining he had family business to attend to, but that he would see her tomorrow if it was convenient. He gave it to Fanning to post and then removed his jacket and cravat and left them on the back of a chair before going to the stable block at the rear of the property.

He pulled the doors open and went inside. There were two empty horse stalls, two carriages, and a harness room. They hadn't kept horses for years, but the place still smelled of hay. The hayloft was empty, as far as he could see. Phantom hay, he thought.

The smaller, two-wheeled cabriolet was at least twenty years old, but still in decent shape. Dab lifted and secured the hood into place. The vehicle was ideal for driving in the city with a single horse. It might even serve well enough for a trip to Standon Cottage, which he was anxious to make. It needed to be sold.

He turned to the larger phaeton. He stepped closer and ran his hand over the back seat. How many times he had ridden there chatting with his parents, looking around at all they passed. There had been so many happy days. If only he'd never spent time with his aunt, how different things would have been.

He sighed deeply as he looked around the dim, spider-web strewn interior of the carriage house. He'd always liked the place; he'd played here, but it was showing signs of serious neglect. Many things were. He needed to fix every bit of it and to get them on firmer financial footing.

He left the doors open and strolled toward the house in time to see a cab creeping by. Dab stopped and stared as the passenger leaned forward to study the house. Unless he was mistaken, it was one of the men working for Chausterfield. So they knew where he was. What was the point of tracking him down … except to lead them to Theo? He scowled at the thought.

The brick exterior of his aunt and uncle's home on John Street was as elegant as Dab remembered it. He felt positively nauseous seeing it again. He climbed from the carriage, helped his mother down, and they went to the front door where he rang the bell without delay. He wanted to get this encounter over with.

Dab's father, Henry Adams, had inherited the baronage, the townhouse and the property in Hertfordshire, yet he'd struggled to maintain it all with meager coffers. George, the younger son by six years, had received the education of his choice and inherited five thousand pounds. With it, he'd become a physician. He'd been content with his life until he met one of the McBride sisters, Florence. Florrie, her friends called her. She was the prettiest McBride girl with lush, auburn hair and a full bosom.

Florrie had her share of suitors, but she liked George best. The only problem was that she required a better life than a mere physician could provide. She had not come from wealth, but she had set her sights on it. She was witty and clever, a vivacious flirt, and she made George feel more alive. He wanted her for his wife, and so he got ambitious. He partnered with an investor, and concocted a laudanum-based tonic, *Doctor G.W. Adam's Remedy for Ladies* that sold well. Well enough for him to give up his practice.

At his first opportunity, he bought out the investor, acquired a small factory for manufacturing the tonic, and threw himself into the marketing and distribution of the product. He had a head for business and his success grew. It pleased Florrie to have wealth and a fine house and nice things, but there was always something else she needed or wanted. Yet, once she got it, it ceased to hold allure for her.

For their entire lives, the Adams brothers had been more competitors than friends, but they'd gotten along well enough. Because George and Florrie had not yet been blessed with children, Dab had frequently been invited to spend time at their home where Florrie doted on him.

Doted, Dab mused bitterly. But his reflection was interrupted by the butler who opened the door.

Dab handed over his card and asked to see his uncle. He wanted to handle this distasteful business one person at a time, starting with the least culpable of the two.

"Please come in, my lord," the butler replied. "My lady," he said with a differential tip of his head to Charlotte. "If you'll follow me, I'll see if he is available." He led them into the parlour, invited them to sit, and left again.

For all his uncle's success, everything, while perfectly clean and polished, had a faded, worn look to it. Perhaps the condition of the house should have served as a clue, but Dab was shocked when his uncle stepped into the room. He looked gaunt, untidy and unsteady from drink.

"Charlotte! Dabney," he exclaimed, stopping inside the doorway. "I am … well, astonished to see you." He came further in. "Delighted, but astonished."

Dab had risen but did not offer his hand.

George glanced at Charlotte's dress and sighed. "I am so terribly sorry about Henry. I wanted to see him again. More than anything, I think."

She nodded. "I know," she said quietly.

Dab felt a stab of surprise at the tenderness in her tone.

"Thank you for telling me of his passing."

"Of course," she said.

George looked at Dab. "You look well. Healthy and handsome. Sit, please."

Dab sat again. "Thank you for seeing us, Uncle George."

"I am thrilled and gratified to see you, but to what do I owe the honor?" The words were pitifully slurred.

"It's not an honor," Dab replied regretfully. "It's more a mission of truth. Reconciling with the past I suppose you could say."

George looked over his shoulder at the butler. "Did you offer our guests something to drink?" he asked.

"I don't care for anything," Charlotte said.

"Nor I," Dab said.

"Well, I do," George said, motioning to the butler who quickly went and poured a glass of whiskey. "Bring the bottle and leave it. And bring some more glasses in case my nephew or sister-in-law decide to join me." He peered at Dab thoughtfully. "It feels to me like it might be a drinking conversation. Am I right?"

"You might be," Dab conceded.

Once his bidding was done, the butler left. George held up his glass. "This is how I reconcile with the past. So, what is it?"

"This will not be easy to hear, sir, but there is something I must say to both you and my aunt."

George grimaced. "Your aunt? You won't be able to do that here. She's been gone for a dozen years."

"Gone?" Charlotte repeated. "Not—"

"Dead?" George asked when she left the utterance unfinished. "No. Not dead. I know because she writes me all the bloody time. Thinks I owe her something. Thinks I treated her badly." He gave an unpleasant bark of laughter. "Can you imagine? That aberrant, deviant woman thinks I treated her badly."

Dab was stunned. *Aberrant. Deviant.* So he knew?

George took a drink and then wiped his mouth with the back of his hand. "I kicked her out is what I did. She didn't get a farthing from me, nor will she."

"But I told you all this," George said to Dab. "I wrote you and your father. Why do you look so surprised?"

Dab shook his head. "I didn't get it. I didn't know."

George looked at Charlotte questioningly before looking back to Dab. "I came home one day and found her with the neighbor's boy." He closed his eyes and exhaled long and slow. "Christ, it made me sick to my stomach. How stupid had I been? I hadn't known. I hadn't seen it. How sodding stupid was I? I kicked her out with her blathering on, crying, making excuses, begging."

George took another drink. "I found solace in a bottle. Ordered the servants to damn well keep her out if they wanted to keep their places. Once I was sober enough, can't say when that was exactly, I wrote to Henry. Told him what happened. I put a letter in there for you too because I wanted you to know how sorry I was. How wrong I'd been. I knew it. I knew it in my gut. I'd been played for a sodding fool."

Dab released a shaky breath. "Maybe I will have a drink," he said.

His uncle gestured to it. "I'd pour, but I'd spill it."

Dab poured a glass and offered it to his mother, who shook her head. She seemed as stunned as he. He took a drink.

George watched him with sunken, haunted eyes. "I blamed you," he admitted. "You were a boy, in our care, and yet I blamed you. But now I know, I know here," he said gesturing to his stomach. "She arranged it all somehow. I'm not wrong, am I?

"No."

George nodded grimly. "To hear her tell it, it was always someone else's fault. Men coming after her. Boys coming after her. Like moths drawn to a flame. But that sort of perversity does not happen unless you arrange it. Unless you set it in motion." He looked at Charlotte. "Did Henry not tell you I wrote?"

"I knew you did," she replied.

"Did he read them?"

She hesitated and then shook her head. "I'm sorry."

He sighed. "Then he bore me a grudge until the day he died," he said. "He never knew how sorry I was." He looked at Dab. "How bloody sorry I am," he muttered. He downed the last of his drink.

"We should go," Charlotte said to her son.

Dab downed his own drink and set the glass down. "Thank you for seeing us, Uncle George."

"I will always see you. I would see you anytime. You've turned into a fine man. Always knew you would be." His voice broke on the last of it and he looked away in embarrassment.

"Are you alright?" Charlotte asked as they rode toward home.

Was he? "I didn't expect that."

"Nor did I." They rode for several blocks in silence before she asked, "Is it worth seeking her out?"

"No." He replied quickly because the answer was obvious, simple, and he meant it. He'd carried a load of anger and resentment for so long but there did not seem to be a vestige of it left. It had been unbelievably sad to see his uncle. All the work the man had put into his business, all the success he had achieved, for what?

Toward Florence, he felt nothing but revulsion, but he wanted to be finished thinking about it. He would not lug shame and resentment around any longer as his cross to bear. He wanted a life, a new life, and he would never allow her near it. "There is someone following us."

"What?" She started to turn around to see, but he stopped her.

"Don't look. They don't realize I'm on to them and I want to keep it that way."

"Who would be following us?"

"Chausterfield's men. The same ones who forced her back inside when we were trying to make our escape."

She released a breath.

"I noticed one of them in a cab creeping by the house earlier. They've obviously followed us today. It's a plain black cab. The driver has a flat hat and white hair. They must be hoping I will lead them to her."

She huffed. "What sort of desperation does this half-brother feel?"

"I have no idea of the specifics, but money is involved."

"Should we try and confront them?"

He pondered a moment. "Can you drive back by yourself?"

"Yes, of course. But why?"

"I want you to drop me off at the pub around the corner. I'll go inside as if I'm meeting someone. I think they'll stay with me. Drive on for a few blocks and then pull over and make sure they're not following you. If they are not, will you do me a favor?"

"Yes. What is it?"

"I want you to go to the Turner home and see Theo. I need to know that she is alright, and she needs to know that I'm being followed. I will not chance seeing her again unless I've managed to shake them."

"What's the address?"

"Denbigh Street, number thirty-nine. It's not far from the crossroads of Vauxhall Bridge Road and Warwick Way."

She nodded.

"Make certain you're not being followed before you go there."

"I will. I will be very careful. As silent and invisible as the breeze. How do you know I wasn't a spy in my youth?"

He chuckled at this playful side of his mother. "Oh, my. What have I unleashed?"

Chapter Fourteen

Mary hurried out to the garden where Theo was on her knees planting chrysanthemums. "Someone is here to see you!"

Theo looked up, surprised by the urgency in Mary's tone. "Is it Dab?"

"It's his mother! Oh, gracious. Get up, my girl. I've told you that you don't need to do that, but... oh, this does look better," she said, looking around the garden.

"And I enjoy it," Theo returned as she got up. "Working in the garden is good for one's soul."

"But you've gotten yourself all dirty," Mary fretted as she bent to brush off Theo's skirt.

Theo chuckled as she stepped around her and started inside, removing her work gloves. "I challenge anyone to accomplish something in a garden and not get dirty." She removed her apron and Mary grabbed it from her as she rushed to keep up.

Theo found Charlotte Adams seated in the drawing room, and there was no doubt about who she was. The resemblance to Dab was striking. "Lady Sonden, hello." She stopped and bobbed a curtsy. "I was working in the garden."

"It's a fine afternoon for it," Lady Sonden replied with a warm smile.

"Please forgive my appearance. I didn't want to take the time to change without—"

Lady Sonden shook her head and waved off the notion. "Your appearance is perfect."

Theo felt awed and a bit conspicuous as she took a seat across from the lady.

"I realize this is without warning or invitation, but Dab asked me to come."

"Oh?"

"Someone has been following him, and he refuses to lead them to you."

Theo's breath hitched.

"He wanted you to know and to make sure you're alright."

"I am. But there is someone following him?"

Charlotte Adams nodded. "He believes it is one of the same men who forced you back inside at the Betrothal Ball. In fact, he feels certain of it."

Theo felt terrible. "I am so sorry to bring this to your doorstep."

"That's not your fault! And I'm very pleased to meet you."

Theo smiled with relief at Lady Sonden's graciousness. "I'm happy to meet you."

"I don't wish to pry, but—" Charlotte leaned forward with a mischievous gleam. "I want to know everything about you," she said conspiratorially.

Theo laughed.

Mary hustled about the kitchen, supposedly helping with tea preparations, but getting in the way more than anything. It was exciting to have Dab's mother show up, and it was thrilling to have a part to play in a great love story. Mary didn't doubt that Theo and Dab would have a great love story, and she and Bert had been there at the beginning. They had helped bring sweet Theo and Dab together.

By the time she led Vera, with the teacart, into the parlour, Theo and Lady Sonden were gabbing like old friends. Theo could charm anyone, but Mary was impressed by Lady Sonden's unpretentiousness. "Is there anything the two of you need?" she asked as tea was served.

"Just for you to join us," Theo said.

"Please," Lady Sonden agreed.

"I wouldn't budge in," Mary resisted.

"Do please join us," Lady Sonden said. "I wanted to meet you, as well. And your husband."

Mary came and sat next to Theo. "Just for a bit, then."

"I was just telling Theo how much we would have loved to have another child," Lady Sonden said. "Theo is so fortunate to have her sisters."

Mary nodded. "Indeed, she is. They sound delightful and I cannot wait to meet them."

"They are overly protective," Theo stated, "—and certain they are right about most things, but, yes, delightful. Usually."

The older ladies chuckled. "We have our son," Mary said. "Thank God. But it's not the same as having a daughter. We had our girl, Amelia, but she got ill when she was thirteen and … passed away. It's never been the same without her."

"I'm sorry," Lady Sonden replied.

Mary smiled wistfully. "I've told Theo all about her."

Theo gave Mary a warm smile and nod.

"We love Freddy, of course, but it's not as easy to be close to a son. Or it wasn't for us, I should say. I was hoping once he was married, I might find that special bond with my daughter-in-law, but she's not keen on the notion. She doesn't even like her own mother overly much."

"That is a shame," Lady Sonden replied.

Mary nodded. "They haven't had children, although I wonder how much we'll be allowed to be involved with them if they are blessed. I fear it won't be as involved as we would like."

"I hope you're wrong about that," Lady Sonden said. "The thought of grandchildren is wonderful."

"Oh, yes," Mary agreed. "Children, grandchildren, great-grandchildren, the neighbor's children. Stranger's children who carol in the street at Christmas."

Theo laughed softly and took hold of Mary's hand and squeezed. Vera appeared, having brought another cup. She poured tea and handed it to Mary. "Thank you, Vera," Mary said.

Vera gave her a nod and subtle wink and left.

"Do try the shortbread," Mary urged the ladies. "It's delicious."

Chapter Fifteen

*T*he following evening, Theo was pleasantly nervous as she left her room. Bert would be escorting her to the Adams home where she would have dinner with Dab and his mother. The dinner had been arranged by Lady Sonden after their completely lovely visit, and Theo could not wait to see Dab again. It was all very clandestine and romantic and exciting.

She heard distressed sounding voices from downstairs. Her sisters' voices! She lifted her skirt and dashed down. Cissy and Laurel were visibly distraught as they spoke with Bert and Mary in the foyer. "What's happened?"

"Oh, Theo," Cissy cried when she saw her. "They've taken Greta!"

"Who? Not Cyrus," Theo pleaded, although it could not be anyone else.

"Yes, Cyrus," Laurel spoke up. "He brought his thugs with him. I wish we could have him arrested!"

"Can your friend Mr. Adams help?" Cissy asked. "He has more power than we do."

Power? What could he do? "What happened exactly?"

"It's our fault," Cissy said. "We went to see Maeve. We knew you weren't there because she'd explained what's happened, but we were so curious and we knew she'd know more than us. We hadn't been there ten minutes when they burst in on us."

"You should have seen Cyrus," Laurel seethed. "The gloating. He announced that he could offer his youngest sister, he actually called her that, immeasurably more than we could, so he would be taking guardianship of her. Well! You can imagine, the three of us stepped in front of her declaring that would happen over our dead bodies. He just laughed," she said bitterly. "And in stepped in his

105

confederates and they took her from us kicking and crying. Meaning Greta was crying. I wanted to kill them. We all did. But we couldn't stop them. They will have bruises and claw marks for some time to come, and I'm glad for every one of them, but we could not stop them."

This was about getting to her, Theo realized dully. This was the ace up his sleeve he'd boasted about. She had been so stupid not to think of it. "Did he say I could exchange myself for her?"

"Not exactly," Laurel prevaricated.

"What exactly?" Theo insisted. "Never mind. I will go get her back. This is about forcing me to do what he wants."

"I feel so foolish and responsible," Cissy uttered. "We shouldn't have gone."

Theo clutched her hand. "She will be fine. I'll assure him I will do as he wishes, so long as he lets her go."

"Theo," Mary uttered with a shake of her head. "Think! Hib will not hurt Greta. They will take excellent care of her, and we will find a way to get her back."

Bert nodded. "I agree. Without sacrificing you."

"Go to Dab, as planned," Mary counseled. "Tell him what's happened and elicit his help."

Laurel nodded. "If you go to Hib, he will seize hold of you and not let you out of his sight until he has you securely married off to one of those men. Devils, all of them."

"Will we be able to get Greta back?" Cissy fretted. "Given his wealth and title and influence?"

Theo shook her head as she thought about it. Cyrus seemed to have the winning hand, but she would not sacrifice her sister.

"At least, speak to Dab first," Mary urged. "We will seek out an attorney tomorrow for guidance on the matter."

No. They didn't understand the trauma Greta had been through. "I will not leave her alone with them, not even for one night," she declared. "I am going, and I will get her released. Cyrus has underestimated me."

"Theo," Bert pleaded.

She felt fire and ice burning at her core. Fire in her belly and ice in her veins. Hurt her sister? She could murder Cyrus given the opportunity! "I would appreciate you taking me there," Theo said to Bert. "But I will take a cab if you would rather not."

"We'll go with you," Cissy said.

Theo shook her head. "Don't be silly. He will not let you in. You know he won't. Mary, Bert," she said, turning to them. "I have to do this. Will you take me?" she asked Bert.

"Yes," he replied. "If you insist. And then I will go let Dab know what's happening. We will speak with an attorney tomorrow … unless he knows of one tonight. We will not abandon you to that bully."

She knew it was true.

Cissy wiped at her eyes and nose with her hanky. "I am so sorry, Theo. I never dreamed—"

"I know," Theo said gently. "It will be alright. I'm ready," she said to Bert.

"Wait," Laurel said with a shake of her head. "This is not the right course of—"

Theo started for the door. She was going. She would not listen to any more arguments.

"My, oh my," Bert said when they arrived at Hib's mansion. He'd spent the entire journey there trying to convince her not to offer to sacrifice herself. What if Chausterfield had the chosen suitor and an officiant on hand to marry them straight away? Tonight? That would complicate matters immeasurably.

"I hope that is not the case," she'd returned, but nothing would dissuade her. She absolutely would not leave Greta at their mercy.

She still felt the fire and ice, but now a heavy weight of dread had also settled into her stomach as she stared at the house. "Cyrus married into money," she said. "Mildred had little else to recommend her but that was enough."

"And yet he is greedy for more," he muttered.

"Even if he hadn't acquired debt, he might still have done this. He was always bitter about my mother and all of us. This must feel like sweet revenge."

Bert shifted to face her, his expression pleading. "I believe with all my heart that you should see Dab first. So does Mary."

"I know," she replied tenderly. "But what could he do? If Cyrus has legal grounds, no one can change that. I've already involved Mr. Adams too deeply."

"*Mister* Adams?" Bert replied wryly.

She sighed. "I couldn't bear it if he was injured because of me. They know where he lives. They were following him. I don't believe there's much Cyrus wouldn't resort to."

"I understand your concern, my dear, but—"

She looked away, prepared to climb down.

"Alright," he gave in. "I can see your mind is made up. At least, let me see you to the door."

She grabbed his hand. "No. Please don't. They won't let you in and I don't want them to be rude to you. I'll be fine."

"Who did you get your stubbornness from?" he teased affectionately.

"Both my parents. In equal measures, I do believe."

"You do them proud, my dear."

She smiled at him and then climbed down and started for the house. The key was to not look back or to think about where she had been going this evening before her sisters showed up. She could not agonize over how close she'd come to a fairy tale romance with a real life Prince Charming. Well, she could agonize over it; she just couldn't let it stop her. She rang the bell.

A butler opened the door and bowed his head to her. "Miss Martel," he said coolly, stepping back.

She entered and he closed the door. How did he know who she was?

"This way, if you please."

She followed him toward the dining hall but met Cyrus and Mildred in the corridor coming out of the salon. "You're here," Cyrus said cheerfully. "Excellent."

"Where is my sister?" she asked without emotion.

"We were just about to have dinner," he said, ignoring her question. "Care to join us? It's beef bourguignon."

"No."

Cyrus's pretense at pleasantness vanished. He gave a jerk of his head to the butler to leave them, and waited until he'd walked on. "I suppose I should thank you. You gave us a merry chase, and, in the end, I ended up with not one but two of you to marry off. Plus, the thrill of winning."

Mildred stepped closer. "How did you do it?" she demanded of Theo.

Theo ignored her. "You will release Greta, or you will end up with neither of us. That I promise you."

"Oh, do you?" He laughed. "Do you really?"

She lifted her chin. Mildred's hand shot up and slapped her across the face and into a wall sconce. Her right cheek bone throbbed with pain.

"You idiot," Cyrus thundered. "Are you mad? Not the face! Never the face!"

Theo turned back in time to see Mildred give her husband a filthy look before storming off. "Get my diamonds back," she called as she went.

Cyrus cursed under his breath.

"Where is Greta?" Theo repeated.

He glowered at her. "She is in the room next to yours," he bit out. "But do not push me, girl." He paused. "Hornsby," he bellowed.

The butler quickly reappeared. So quickly that he could not have been far, undoubtedly listening to everything.

"Take her up," Cyrus ordered. "Where I said, as I said."

"My lord," Hornsby said with a dip of his head.

Theo puzzled over Cyrus's cryptic instructions as she followed Hornsby down the corridor, up the stairs and down the hallway. She resisted the urge to touch her throbbing cheekbone. He stopped at a door, opened it and motioned her inside. "Which one is my sister in?"

"Theo?" Greta called from the room to the right.

Theo pushed by the butler and went to the door and tried the knob, but it was locked. She turned to the maddeningly impassive servant. "May I speak with her first?"

With a bored expression, he gestured more elaborately to the room she'd been assigned.

"I can't open it," Greta called. "It's locked."

"So her room is right there next to mine, but you're refusing to let me see her?"

"I have my orders, Miss Martel. If you would please," he said, gesturing at her designated room.

"My room is next door," Theo called back to Greta. She donned her best imperious expression and stepped past the butler and into the room. Immediately, she saw a door that had to adjoin Greta's room. As she started for it, the door to her room slammed shut. She turned back to look at it as it was locked. Heartless bullies! The door adjoining Greta's room was also locked. Theo banged on it in frustration.

"Did they find you, too?" Greta asked mournfully from the other side.

"No. I came for you." Theo went to the door to the balcony. It was not locked. "The balcony," she called. Greta rushed out onto her balcony at the same time Theo stepped out. They gravitated as close to one another as possible, which was still seven or eight feet away. "He is so deplorable," Greta declared. She gasped, noticing Theo's cheek. "Did he hit you?"

"No, Mildred did. She is equally deplorable. Are you alright?"

Greta nodded but she looked miserable. "They didn't hurt me. Mildred didn't utter one word to me. She just studied me as if I was some unusual variety of moth."

Theo looked around for a path of escape, but there was nothing to climb down, and the ground was too far away to jump. "There must be a way to get to you."

"You can't," Greta said.

Something about the words *you can't* made Theo want to lift a brow, fold her arms, and prove that she could, as a matter of fact. She returned to her room. The furniture was heavy and there was nothing long and straight except the freestanding mirror. Theo tried to move it, but it was heavy. Too heavy. The base of the wood framed mirror slid into a wood and metal base. She braced the sides, tugged upwards and it gave. It could slide out, but it was heavy.

She took a breath and heaved. It came out, but she stumbled backwards drunkenly and nearly lost control of it before she managed to steady it. She would have to either walk it or drag it. She tipped it and moved one side and then the other, walking it inch by inch. It was slow, but it was working. Maneuvering it over the doorway to the balcony was a challenge, but she managed it.

"Theo," Greta objected.

"It's worth a try," Theo returned.

There was a knock on Greta's door. She glanced toward it. "They said they would bring dinner."

"Go," Theo urged. She set the mirror against the side of the house and went back inside to her door to listen. When she heard her sister's door close again, she waited a moment to see if she would be served next and then she knocked. "Are you bringing me dinner?" she called. After several moments, she heard a female voice on the other side of the door.

"I was told not to. That you didn't want it."

"I do. I'm hungry. Will ... will you, please?"

"I'll fetch it, Miss."

Theo looked behind her. The missing mirror was not obvious from the doorway. She went back onto the balcony. Greta was on hers. "They're going to bring me a tray. In the meantime." She went back to her earlier effort.

"What are you thinking? Not climbing over?"

"If it will reach, yes. If not ... oh, well. There went your nice mirror."

"No. You cannot. You will fall and kill yourself."

"We don't even know if we can get it in place. Let's just see."

Greta thrust her hands on her hips. "We?"

Theo maneuvered the mirror to the railing, tipped it and began to force it over, using the railing as leveraging. "Be ready to grab it, if you can."

Greta started to object, but the mirror was already in the air, midway between them. She stretched her arms out as it came toward her. "I've got it," she called, "but I don't think it will reach." Theo kept a grip and Greta eased her side down. She shook her head. "I only have an inch over here."

It was the same on Theo's side. Climbing over it would not be impossible, but if it slipped at all, which it might, she would fall. She looked at the ground again. It was probably thirty feet down.

"No," Greta repeated. "It is too dangerous."

Theo tested the give of the railing and found it sturdy. If she moved very slowly and the mirror didn't slide, she would be fine. She had good balance. Not as good as before the accident, but still fine. Not bad, anyway. She looked at her anxious sister. "How's the railing on your side? Sturdy?"

"No, Theo! I forbid it."

Theo gave her a look.

Greta scowled. "I will push this mirror to the ground before I let you try and traipse across and break your neck."

Theo's look turned pleading. "Please, don't. I swear, I won't attempt it if I truly believe I can't make it work."

Greta looked indecisive.

"I'll wait for my dinner," Theo said, turning for the room.

"Theo," Greta cried.

"It will be fine," Theo said, heading inside. She prayed she would not hear the crash of the mirror as she waited at the door. A light knock precipitated the turning of the lock and the door opened. A maid stood there with a tray. "Here you are, Miss."

"Thank you," Theo said as she took it. "I need to see my sister," she said pleadingly. "Won't you please unlock the door between our rooms?"

"I can't," the maid replied with a pained expression and a shake of her head. "I am sorry, but I can't. I'd lose my position."

Theo sighed silently and nodded. "Thank you for the tray."

"I am sorry," the maid said again. She closed the door and locked it.

Theo carried the tray back to the balcony. "I'll slide this over first and—"

"Theo! No! I nearly lost you once."

Theo put the tray on the mirror and slid it halfway over.

Greta frowned and folded her arms.

"If you won't help, it will be more difficult," Theo said calmly.

"I am not encouraging this," Greta stated.

Theo smiled and then laughed. "That sounded just like Mamma."

Greta softened. "It did, didn't it?"

Theo nodded. "The mirror is heavy," she reasoned, "and I'll be so, so careful. I swear it. I will not fall and kill myself."

"You cannot promise that."

"I promise that I will move slowly and if I feel the tiniest bit of movement, I will get back down."

Greta frowned, but leaned over, got hold of the tray and slid it toward her. "I am taking this only because I can send it back when you've regained your senses."

"Fair enough." As Greta carried it into the room, Theo considered how to proceed. She went back in her room for a chair and brought it back. She removed her skirt.

Greta reemerged from the room, shocked at what she saw. "What are you—"

"Take this," she said sending her skirt over.

Greta grabbed it. "We need a rope between us," she said. "In case you start to slip. I'll either catch you or ... you're damn well not falling without me this time." She gasped. "I know," she exclaimed before she dashed back inside. She was back momentarily with a silken cord with tasseled ends. "From the bed curtains," she said excitedly. "But we need two of them tied together, don't we? And a chair on this side." She hurried back in without waiting for an answer.

Theo climbed up on the chair and experienced a moment of vertigo that made her climb back down, struggling for breath. She wasn't sure she could do this, but then Greta was back with two cords tide together, and so proud of herself. It seemed like ages since the two of them had been together. Greta tossed an end of the rope onto the mirror and Theo retrieved it and pulled over the rest of it.

"Tie it on your wrist," Greta said. "Tightly."

Theo sat on the chair and managed it using her knees and feet and teeth. How absurd looking she was! "That's as tight as I can get it," she said, tossing the far end back to Greta.

"I feel a little better," Greta said as she began securing it around the railing. "I'll brace the mirror on this side."

Theo steadied her nerves and stood on the chair again, fighting a rebellion of abject terror.

"If it slips at all," Greta uttered.

"I know. *Shh.*" Theo shook out her hands, breathed in and out, and bent to place her hands on either side of the mirror and one knee on the mirror. It had a sturdy wood backing, so it would surely support her weight.

"Don't look down," Greta coached.

"Greta, stop! When you tell me not to look down, all I want to do is look down. I have to concentrate." She lifted her foot off the chair and brought the knee in front of the other. She'd felt no movement of the mirror and she was committed to the action now. She was squarely on top of the mirror, hands and knees and all the shivering rest of her.

"Oh my God," Greta muttered. "This is the stupidest thing we have ever done."

"I am going to kill you," Theo muttered.

"Good. Come over here and kill me. Or crawl back and I'll kill myself. I just need you to be safe."

Theo inched one hand up, and then the other, and then her back knee. She inched the other hand up, the back knee, and then the other. She was halfway there. Slow and easy. No sudden jerks. This truly was incredibly foolish. She reached the other balcony and Greta's hands closed around her arms. Now all she had to do was to climb over without making the mirror slide. "This really is the stupidest thing we've ever done," she agreed.

"Don't start us laughing now," Greta warned.

Theo took another breath and brought one leg around. She touched the seat of the chair and then carefully finished the trek. Greta threw herself in her arms and they held one another. It was impossible to tell which of them was shaking the most. Greta untied the rope from Theo's wrist, and they made their way inside, Greta dragging the chair behind her.

"Sit," Greta said.

Theo sat, shaken in the aftermath of the climb. "I'm so glad there's wine," Theo said, reaching for the carafe. Her hands shook as she poured.

Greta plunked down in the other chair. "You are insane."

Theo held up her glass. "Bear in mind, we are nuts from the same tree."

Greta poured herself a glass and they caught their breath and drank wine until they'd calmed. "Did Sissy and Laurel come for you?"

"Yes."

"We shouldn't have gone home but I imagine they would have found me at Sissy's eventually."

Theo nodded, because it was possible. "I didn't even consider that he might make a grab for you."

"Neither did we." Greta lifted the lid off the plate to see what lay beneath. Beef bourguignon. "Looks delicious." She looked at Theo. "I'm glad we can eat together, but was my company worth risking your life?"

"Yes. Besides, it helped me work up quite an appetite."

They laughed and began to eat. "Tell me all about your new friend. Maeve said he is the most handsome man she has ever clapped eyes on."

"Yes, but that's the least of who he is."

"Tell me."

Theo drew breath but was stymied. How did she even begin?

"Is it that difficult?"

"No, it's just … he's so many things. Protective and kind and—"

"Start with the night it happened," Greta interrupted. "The Betrothal Ball."

Theo searched for the right place to begin.

Greta laughed. "Why is it so difficult?"

"Because I want to do it justice. It was … magical." She paused. "Imagine for a moment that Cinderella had a younger sister. The story happened, just as we know it—"

"Except for her having the younger sister, you mean?"

"Yes. Except for that. Cinderella comes home from the ball in rags, the very same as when her sister last saw her, but she's ablaze with love and adoration."

Greta smirked. "That is very dramatic."

"The story is dramatic. It's been the adventure of her life. She was dressed in finery and taken to a ball where she met the prince and danced with him. She was made to feel special by someone who was revered."

"I do know the story."

Theo ignored the interruption. "The sister asks where she's been all evening and Cinderella wants to explain what happened."

"You're saying your ball was that magical?"

"Minus the fairy godmother," Theo teased. "Actually, that's not true. Because Mary was there. I had a fairy godmother and godfather."

"Enough fairy tales. I want to hear every single detail from the second you stepped foot in the ballroom to the last. Right until this moment."

Theo reached for her sister's hand and clutched it tightly. "I have missed you so much.

Greta's eyes filled. "I've missed you."

Theo nearly asked why she'd been avoiding her, but she didn't want to go to a dark place. So, for the next hour, they ate and sipped wine, and Theo shared everything. It was liberating to admit it all. Confidences that could be shared nowhere else could be entrusted to a sister. Entrusted, held, understood, and even treasured because of the secrecy.

Afterwards, Greta talked about life at Cissy's, complete with anecdotes of both their elder sisters, brothers-in-law, and all the children. Living with their eldest sister seemed to be exactly what she had needed. And being with Greta was something Theo had needed. Together they would find a way to outsmart Cyrus.

It wasn't until they were in bed that night, facing one another, both of them in their shifts since neither had a proper nightgown, that Theo finally asked. "Why have you avoided me these last months?"

Greta's face darkened. "Can we not talk about it? Please?"

"I need to know. Was it something I did?"

Greta looked crestfallen. "No!"

"Then what?"

Greta sighed heavily. "What do you remember of the accident?"

It was the one subject they had not talked about. "The rain," Theo said. "The miserably cold, incessant rain. The roof was leaking. We were focused on that, but then something happened. The coach swerved back and forth. And then … nothing. It all goes black."

"You don't know how lucky you are."

Theo gripped her sister's arm. "Tell me."

Greta turned onto her back and stared at the ceiling. "It was miserable. We weren't sure how we were going to make it all the way to London. Mamma and Rose sat on one side and you and I sat facing the back."

Theo nodded. Their mother had never been able to ride on the backwards-facing side. It made her nauseous.

"The reason the coach started to swerve was because another carriage had appeared on the road in front of it. It was the Bexleys. Mr. and Mrs. Bexley and Mattias, the middle son. Our driver veered to avoid them … b-but went too far. The Bexley's watched in disbelief as our coach began to tip. They said it happened so fast. It was the back wheel or both right wheels. The icy road and the weight of the coach." She released a shuddering breath. "The horses panicked, trying to stop it from going over."

Theo nearly gasped for breath. She'd been holding it without realizing it.

"We knew what was happening," Greta continued. "But we could do nothing. You were next to the door, and you got it open even though we were already tipping. We were screaming. The horses were screaming. You'd grabbed my wrist. *We have to jump,* you shouted. *Grab Rose,* you said. But we'd tipped too far. It was too late. I thought we were all dead."

Theo was sensing movement and remembering. She'd been terrified. "So did I," she realized.

Greta looked at her sharply. "You remember?"

Theo sat straight up. She did. She remembered Mamma clutching Rose tightly, her eyes wide with fear and regret. Rose's face was buried against her.

Greta sat, too. "I didn't grab her," she admitted brokenly as tears streamed down her face. "I reached for you. And then we were falling and flying."

Falling and flying. That was what it had felt like.

"The sound of the coach falling and hitting was the most terrible sound I could have ever imagined," Greta said just above a whisper." She shivered. "You and I ... we'd landed on the edge of the road." Greta shivered and wiped her face with both hands. "The road was so slippery. It's as if we weren't supposed to survive. I couldn't hold on, but then Mr. Bexley was there. He grabbed my wrists and he hauled me to safety. But you had slipped and fallen to the ledge below. You hit your head and ... blood was coming from it. So much blood, Theo. The rain kept falling and ... there was so much blood."

Theo realized how terrible it must have been for Greta. The coach had disappeared over the side taking her mother and baby sister with it, and then she had fallen, as well.

"They tried to get me into their carriage, but I wouldn't go. I couldn't stop crying and screaming. Mr. Bexley and Mattias got a rope and Mattias climbed down to the ledge. It was so dangerous, but he tied the rope around you, and they got you up. You were limp. The back and side of your head was—"

Theo rubbed her arms.

"Wet with blood." She took a few breaths. "They took you to Doctor Lewis. I held you."

"And the others?" It came out as a whisper.

Greta shook her head. "You know the cliffs. There was no life below. No movement. No way of surviving that. Of course, we couldn't get to them from there, but we went as soon as you were with the doctor. There must have been a hundred people helping by then, despite the sleet." Greta released another shaky breath and wiped her face. "I was told they all died on impact. Even the horses. There was no suffering, other than the terror they had to have known as they fell."

It grew quiet except for their breathing.

"Mamma and Rose were buried the next afternoon in the family plot. You were made ready, and we left for the city the following morning. Dr. Lewis told me you might never wake."

"How terrible for you," Theo grieved softly. "Going through all of that alone."

"It was terrible for you, too."

"I still don't understand why you avoided me once I'd recovered."

Silence.

"I didn't save Rose," Greta uttered.

Theo grabbed hold of her. "You couldn't have! Mamma held her so tightly. As if she could keep her from harm."

Greta shook her head. "I—"

"Listen to me! You could not have saved her, any more than you could have saved Mamma or the horses or the poor driver. It was a horrible accident. You are not to blame for anything."

Greta began crying again and Theo gathered her in her arms and cried with her.

Chapter Sixteen

*T*heo and Greta failed to hear the light knock or the key turning in the lock the following morning. It was the maid's gasp that woke them.

"How—" was all the poor girl managed to utter as she stood there with a breakfast tray, her mouth ajar.

Theo pulled herself upright trying to clear her mind. "Oh. Yes. Well, I was desperate to see my sister," she said in a morning rasp. "Would you believe I leapt from one balcony to the other?"

The maid was aghast. "You might have been killed!"

"I realize that," Theo replied sheepishly. "I have been known to act first and think later."

Greta sat and held the covers to herself. "It's true," she said. "Our mother was forever scolding her about it."

"Perhaps you could simply unlock the door between our rooms. It would save me from breaking my neck and it would be our secret. We'd be ever so grateful."

If angst was an indication, the maid seemed to be considering it. She walked over to the table and set down the tray before placing the breakfast things and collecting the dishes from dinner.

"You realize we're being held prisoner?" Greta asked.

The girl fumbled to retrieve the right key. "They cannot know," she pleaded.

"No, of course not," Theo agreed.

"We will never tell," Greta pledged. "In fact, *you* don't even know the door is unlocked. Theo is brilliant when it comes to getting in locked doors. She's always been mischievous like that."

Theo and Greta exchanged a glance as the door between rooms was unlocked. "I have, haven't I?" Theo murmured.

"I am going around to bring your breakfast into your room," the maid told Theo.

Theo nodded. "Thank you."

The maid picked up the tray and left, and the girls gave each other an excited smile. "Step one," Theo whispered.

"Step two is using the chamber pot," Greta said, swinging her legs around. "And then getting that mirror put back into place." She rose and smirked. "Would you believe I leapt."

"I didn't say I did. I asked if she'd believe it." Theo started to her room as her bedroom door was opened.

"Your cheek is bruised," Greta warned.

Theo closed the door between their rooms as the maid appeared with a polite, "Good morning, Miss."

"Good morning," Theo returned for the benefit of anyone who might be in the hallway.

The maid came in and set out her breakfast, unquestionably noticing the missing chair and mirror. "The master wishes to see you after breakfast. I'll give you time to eat and then help you dress."

"Thank you. What is your name?"

"It's Mabel, Miss."

"Thank you, Mabel."

"You're welcome, Miss Martel."

There was a gleam in Mabel's eye. As she left the room, Theo could have sworn she was walking taller with just a hint of swagger. Theo smiled, but then flinched at the ache in her cheek.

An hour later, Theo was shown into Cyrus's study, although he did not arrive for another half hour. When he did, he was humming. His demeanor was cheery, as if he hadn't a care in the world. *Mister game player*, she thought. *Two can play that game.*

He rounded the desk. "Sorry to keep you waiting. Something came up."

She gave him a friendly, phony smile. "Please don't feel badly. You haven't delayed me from any other appointments. I kept the entire morning open for you."

His smile dimmed as he considered her. He pulled back his chair and sat. He put his elbows on the desk and clasped his hands tightly. There seemed to be a lot of tension in those hands for someone without a care in the world. She made it a point to stay relaxed, or at least to give the appearance of being relaxed.

"Put something on that cheek," he said grimly. "Cosmetics or what not. Whatever women do to cover up bruises."

"I've never had to cover up a bruise on my face before and I don't have any cosmetics. Does Mildred have any I could borrow?"

His eyes narrowed. "Pugh will be here later today and the two of you will make arrangements for a ceremony. I expect a superb performance from you. Do not disappoint me. If you do, you know full well who will pay."

She held his gaze. She was trapped and they both knew it, but she would not give him the satisfaction up seeing her flinch or squirm.

He leaned back in the chair. "How did you do it?" he asked conversationally. "How did you coerce none other than the famed Dabney Adams into claiming you?"

She tried to look earnest as she gave a shrug of bafflement. "But that's just the thing; I have no idea how it came about. I was put in the salon to wait for the announcements and … the next thing I knew, a young man came into the room and gave me Mr. Adam's calling card. He said there'd been a change of plans. I thought you were behind it."

Cyrus looked confused and then suspicious. "You are lying."

"Why would I? How would I have gotten his card? I didn't even know who Lord Sonden was. Afterwards, I was whisked away by him and his friends and installed in a home with a nice older couple named Gregson. I was well treated but … obviously perplexed by the change in plans."

His face hardened." Get out of my sight, you duplicitous chit."

She flashed a hurt look, and then rose and left the room. She did not give in to a satisfied grin until she was nearly back to her room.

She went to tell Greta about the meeting, but her younger sister wasn't in the room. Theo experienced a moment of painful remorse for toying with Cyrus. She had come up with her story and she would not stray from it, but she had to be very careful when he could retaliate against Greta. She had to remember why she was here and be very careful.

~~~

Dab paced around his father's old room. It was empty and there was no reason for being there, other than he couldn't stay still and he'd already been in and around most every other room in the house. Once again, Chausterfield had Theo in his clutches and, this time, he'd nabbed the youngest Martel as additional leverage.

Dab would have stormed Chausterfield's residence, except that it would serve no purpose other than to warn the man. He craved action but it needed to be coupled with deliberation. Getting Theo and Greta released was the only goal. He had rallied his friends, and everyone was doing what they could to help.

JG was on his way to speak to his godfather, a solicitor, to find out what legal rights Cyrus Martel had regarding Greta. Nigel had gone to his Aunt Rosemont because she knew a magistrate who could be called on for advice. Hugh was seeking guidance from a professor of law at Cambridge, and Jonathan was ready to supply whatever assistance he could. Bert and Mary wanted to help. His own mother wanted to help. But what could any of them do?

"Theo," he said under his breath. *If Chausterfield had hurt her in any way.* Dab's hands clenched into fists.

~~~

Charles Pugh arrived at three o'clock that afternoon. Theo had done her best to cover the bruise using rice powder, however his gaze went right to it when she entered the salon. She could tell that

123

the sight of it disturbed him. "Miss Martel. I hope I find you well," he asked her searchingly.

"Very well, Mr. Pugh. Thank you. And yourself?"

"I'm well."

"Would you care to sit? They'll bring tea soon."

"Tea sounds wonderful, but I feel a particular restlessness this afternoon. Could we perhaps take a stroll before tea? It's cloudy and muggy. If we can get some fog and a spot of rain, it will be perfect London weather."

She smiled. She really did like Charles Pugh. "A walk sounds nice."

"Good. Around the block then."

They left the room and started down the corridor. She resisted the urge to look into the next room. She had no doubt that either Cyrus or Mildred had an ear pressed to the wall listening to every word they had spoken. She suspected Charles knew it as well.

"You are originally from Dover, I understand," he said, making light conversation.

"Yes."

"Do you miss it? The salty sea air?"

She nodded. "Yes." The front door was opened for them, and they went through. They didn't speak again until they were out of possible earshot of anyone from the house. Staring straight ahead, he asked. "Did he hit you?"

"No."

He glanced at her. "I would like to understand what is happening."

"I believe you," she said softly. "But I am not at liberty to say. I would if I could."

They walked in silence until they rounded the block. "I refuse to be part of a forced marriage, Theo. May I call you Theo?"

"Yes. That's what my friends and family call me."

"I want to be your friend." He stopped and turned to her, glancing behind to make sure they had not been followed. "I can take you away from here. Now. Today. Take you anywhere you want to go. I was a fool to be a party to this. I'd hoped you were amenable, at first, and you are so lovely. I wanted you to choose me, but how much of that was competition with Pearce? That makes me ashamed to admit."

She shook her head, excusing him.

"This is against your will, so why don't I remove you from this place?"

She wished she could tell him the truth.

"Is it a question of having no place to go that's safe from him?"

"No."

"Then what? I know he hit you. Or she did."

How she wished she could blurt it all out.

"He's holding something over you. I am good at business, which means I am good at reading people."

She glanced behind her and then started forward with a slow step. He stayed alongside her, both of them looking straight ahead.

"Trust me to help you, Theo. What's he got?"

"It's not a what," she admitted. "It's a who. My younger sister, Greta." She glanced over and saw that he was shocked.

"Where is she?" he asked as calmly as if they were discussing the weather.

"Cyrus and his hired men ... there were two of them at the ball. I don't know if you realized that or not."

"No," he replied with confusion.

"Anyway, they snatched her away from my elder sisters and brought her here. The message was clear; if I refused to be used as a pawn to pay off these debts of his, whatever they are, she would. That's why I returned; but I think he means to use us both." She stopped abruptly and turned to him. "Does he have a legal right to enforce a guardianship on her?"

"How old is she?"

"Twenty."

"That doesn't seem right to me," he replied with a shake of his head. "If she was thirteen or fourteen, perhaps." He thought about it. "Martel removed her forcibly?"

"Kicking and screaming. Both our elder sisters and a friend tried to stop them, but they couldn't."

"He brings her here," he said, "sending a message to you that you'd better damn well get in line or else. Do I have that right?"

She nodded. "Yes." Had she made a mistake in confiding in him?

"I understand," he said quietly. They walked on, neither of them speaking for the rest of the block. "Do you have any special requests for our ceremony?"

She felt a sudden chill. He had asked it so calmly and dispassionately. So he knew the truth and didn't care? If so, she had made a terrible mistake. Should she beg him not to tell Cyrus?

"Anyone you'd like in attendance?" He continued. "A bridesmaid perhaps?"

Comprehension dawned and she looked at him. He looked back at her and winked. Her heart thudded heavily. She had not made a mistake in trusting him. "As a matter of fact," she said. "I would love to have my younger sister as a bridesmaid."

"You have a younger sister? I had no idea."

She smiled as they turned the corner and the house came into view again. A carriage was in front, and Greta was being helped out followed by Mildred. Theo was so relieved to see her sister. She'd feared they had installed her elsewhere to keep them apart. "That's her now."

He offered Theo his arm, and she gladly took hold. Mildred glanced over and saw them at that moment. She stopped and stared. Charles threw his hand up in greeting to her. Mildred waved back hesitantly and entered the house.

"Dreadful woman, isn't she?" he said under his breath. "I could almost feel sorry for Martel if I didn't despise him so."

She nodded in complete agreement.

"Hello, hello," Charles said cheerfully as they met Cyrus and Mildred in the foyer. There was no sign of Greta.

"Good afternoon," Cyrus returned. "Did you have a nice walk?"

Charles looked to Theo to supply the answer. She smiled." In this perfect London weather? Of course, we did. How could we not?"

The response pleased Cyrus. "Tea is being served," he said to Charles. "Join us."

"I'd love to. Will Greta join us as well?"

A shocked silence fell over the older couple.

"Theo just mentioned she had a younger sister when we saw you walking in with her, Lady Chausterfield," Charles continued as if he hadn't noticed any sort of reaction on their part. "I had no idea." He looked at her affectionately. "There's still so much we have to learn about one another."

She nodded.

Mildred caught the butler's eye and gestured, and he left with a brisk step, hopefully to fetch Greta. He stayed aware of what was going on. Mildred led the way into the drawing room, Theo followed, and the men trailed after her. They sat and were served as the men began discussing some substantial change in banking, something to do with the gold standard. Theo listened halfheartedly, wondering how their situation had altered with Charles Pugh on their side.

Greta entered, looking fresh and beautiful in a gown the colours of a glorious sunset.

The men stood.

"This is my youngest sister," Cyrus said. "Greta."

Charles bowed his head. "An honor, Miss Greta."

She gave a graceful curtsy as a soft blush bloomed in her face. "It is an honor to meet you, Mr. Pugh."

"Join us, my dear," Charles said pleasantly to Greta.

"Thank you," she returned. She walked to a chair and sat, as did the men. A maid served her, and Greta nodded her thanks.

"That is a lovely gown," Theo complimented her.

Greta smiled. "Our sister-in-law took me to the dressmaker's shop. I was measured for something new, but she had ready-made gowns as well. This one only needed a few alterations."

"It looks wonderful on you," Theo said. "I love the colour."

"So have you just arrived in town," Charles asked, "or have you been enjoying the season?"

Cyrus stiffened.

"I have not experienced much of the season this year," Greta replied easily. "Has it been an enjoyable one?"

127

Charles grinned. "I would not be the one to ask. Fancy balls are not my cup of tea, you could say."

"I suppose business is," Greta returned.

"Yes. It keeps me busy."

"I hope to learn about it one day."

"Be careful what you wish for. It might bore you senseless."

"I very much doubt that. Theo has not been bored senseless."

"Indeed not," Theo agreed.

Charles gave Theo a warm smile before looking back to Greta. "Theo and I would both like for you to serve as her bridesmaid."

Greta's smile turned even brighter. "Oh, yes! We always planned on being one another's bridesmaid."

"When are you thinking?" Cyrus asked Charles with an edge to his tone. Control of the conversation had been out of his grasp, and he did not like it.

Charles looked at Theo. "Could you be ready day after tomorrow? Or would that be rushing you too much?"

"No, that would be fine. I'm ready."

Charles smiled and looked at Cyrus and Mildred. "We decided on our walk that an informal ceremony would be best for us. If you have no objections?"

"None at all," Cyrus replied expansively.

Mildred gave a rare smile that did not look quite believable. "Quite fitting," was her only comment.

Charles nodded. "Yes. Good. That settles it then. I will make all the arrangements. Shall we say … three o'clock in the afternoon?"

Theo nodded and attempted a smile. She hoped she'd pulled it off. She was beginning to feel panicked and a bit queasy.

When Charles Pugh said his goodbyes an hour later, Cyrus stood to walk him out. "Ladies, I'll be back," he said, although his cool gaze was on Theo. Almost like a warning.

He ought to have been pleased that arrangements were made, and that she'd put on a good show, as far as he knew, but he detested her. No matter what. No matter how this turned out or what she did. And she detested him with as much or even greater fervor. She looked at Greta. "Tell me about the dress shop," she said.

"It was very nice. It's the same one you went to for your ballgowns. They're sending some things for you this afternoon."

"How lovely."

"Where are my diamonds?" Mildred asked Theo sharply.

Theo looked at her. "They are perfectly safe, Mildred. They will be returned to you as soon as I'm able to get to them. I never expected the developments that occurred, as you must know. Had I planned on coming here, I would have packed properly and returned them to you. I never planned on keeping them."

Mildred narrowed her eyes at the girl. "I think you *planned* quite a bit. You may have pulled the wool over my husband's eyes—"

Cyrus stepped back into the room, silencing her. "That went surprisingly well," he commented, although suspicion rang through the words.

Theo shrugged lightly. "I realized today how very much I like him."

"I'm glad to hear it. However, just in case you are trying to lull me into complacency and then pull some trick card, just know that will not happen. You caused me great difficulty before. I will not allow it to happen again. So, you will both be restricted to your rooms. You will be brought your meals and whatever else you require, within reason. You may converse on the balcony if you wish. But until we leave this house for the ceremony, you will know no freedom."

Theo considered and then nodded. "You will get no more arguments from me," she said evenly.

Cyrus looked pointedly at Greta.

"Or me," Greta added innocently.

He seemed satisfied. "Pugh will inform me of the place for the ceremony, and I will bring the two of you."

Theo did her utmost to remain expressionless.

"Yes, brother," Greta said with a straight face.

His eyes narrowed momentarily and then he gave a dismissive gesture. "You may return to your rooms."

The girls rose and left. They walked at an unhurried pace with composed faces, although they could hardly wait to come together. A maid followed a few feet behind them, and the butler probably watched them all, to make certain they didn't try to bolt.

Upstairs, they both filed inside their own room like a brave if condemned inmate. Greta first, and then the door was locked behind her. Once they were inside their rooms, and the maid had walked away, they wasted no time. They met at the adjoining door.

Theo was the first to speak. "Brother?"

"And I said it with a straight face!"

Theo laughed. "Did you see his face?"

Greta nodded, smiling broadly. "Like he realized he'd swallowed a bug. I think I'm going to say it from now on. Good morning, brother. Did you sleep well, brother?" She paused. "But seriously, what happened today? Mr. Pugh is not at all what I was expecting."

"Today was not what I expected either." Theo pulled Greta close to whisper. "He *knows* and he is on our side."

Greta pulled back to look at her, hardly daring to hope, and Theo nodded. "He knows?" she mouthed.

Theo nodded again, but then she looked around the room nervously. "Does it feel like someone is spying on us?"

Rather than answer, Greta went and looked under her bed. "No one there," she reported. She went to the wardrobe and looked inside. She shut the doors and turned back with a shake of her head. "I want to hear every word exchanged between the two of you."

"Let me check my room first." Theo went and conducted a quick search.

"Tell me!"

Theo acquiesced, starting with her morning conversation with Cyrus and finding Greta had been removed.

Greta considered all of it. "What a turn of events, but we still don't know what will happen day after tomorrow."

It was true, but Theo's heart was beating so fast and with such hope. "But it feels like we have a friend on our side who can effect a change in the outcome of things."

"I hope so, but I honestly do not see a way for it to work out and for us to go free."

Theo didn't see it either, but she believed that Charles would try.

"He was so nice," Greta remarked. "And handsome. I wasn't expecting that. You hadn't said."

"He's been nice all along," Theo admitted, "But he surprised me today. He was compassionate ... and insightful. Unless I am being fooled, which I don't think I am, he was perfectly on cue. Strong and impressive. Clever. Believable."

Greta was nodding. "Let me ask you this," she said solemnly. "I believe he will try, but if he does not figure a way out of this mess, could you marry him and be happy?"

Theo sighed, but then considered before replying. "Between Sir Amos Pearce or Charles Pugh, the choice was easy. It was Charles. I'd decided that much at the Betrothal Ball. But then I met Dab. If I hadn't, perhaps I could have gone along and been content. But content isn't happy. It's not in love."

"Are you certain you're in love with Dabney Adams? Without a shadow of a doubt? I'm not challenging, I'm just asking."

"Yes," Theo replied calmly. "That's not to say he feels the same about me or that we would have gotten married. But now I've felt that power and magic that Mamma always spoke of and that our parents had. Even if Dab doesn't feel the same about me, I want it, the real thing. I also want it for you. Cyrus should not get to choose our fate."

Greta nodded. "You're right."

"I like Charles Pugh," Theo said. "Very much. But I do not love him and I will not marry him. Unless I am forced against my will." Unless they threatened to hurt Greta.

"But how can Mr. Pugh pull it off?" Greta asked softly.

Theo wished she knew. "Other people care too, you know. I know that our sisters are trying. And Bert and Mary. And Dab. I don't doubt for a moment that they are all doing what they can for us."

Greta nodded and then wandered out to the balcony, where a ray of sunshine broke through to shine on her as if it was a pleasure to do so.

Chapter Seventeen

A s Theo rode next to Greta and across from Cyrus and Mildred, she did not have to play the nervous bride. She was nervous and it was conceivable she was about to be a bride. "Where are we going?" she asked since no information had been forthcoming.

"To your wedding," Cyrus replied glibly.

"I meant where specifically? To a church?"

"No. We're going to your future residence. Pugh wanted it held there. Of course, it's far more customary to have the wedding in the bride's home, but this hasn't been the usual affair, has it?"

She looked out the window. Hib was so puffed up; it was a wonder they could all fit in the carriage. It was little wonder since he had won. Whatever debt he had to Charles Pugh was being wiped off the books today.

"Is this it?" Greta asked when the carriage stopped.

"Yes," Cyrus replied.

"It's beautiful," Greta said to Theo.

The house was beautiful. Very grand. Charles Pugh had made a good deal of money and he clearly enjoyed showing it off.

"Let's go," Cyrus said.

Mildred was helped from the carriage first and then Greta. Cyrus gave Theo a sharp look and got out, and Theo followed, but only because she had absolutely no choice in the matter. Continuing toward the front door felt a bit like walking to a scaffold for her execution.

Was this it? Was a wedding ceremony about to take place? Had Charles Pugh even tried to find a way around it or had his concern and his assurances all been a ruse?

As the front door was opened to admit them, Theo felt Greta take her arm in support. Inside, Charles stood speaking with an officious looking man in a black robe. Theo felt unsteady. Charles seemed calm and contented. Had she been utterly taken in by him? Had he ever intended on helping her? What about Greta? Would he simply stand by while Cyrus traded her to the next man he owed money to?

Over her dead body!

"Good afternoon," Charles greeted all of them with a gracious smile.

"Good afternoon," Cyrus returned.

"Good afternoon, Mr. Pugh," Greta said with a dip of her head.

Charles caught Theo's gaze and gave her a different sort of smile and nod, one that was probably supposed to appear supportive. It didn't work. She felt frozen.

Charles looked at Cyrus. "I believe you and I have a bit of business to attend to first thing," he said pleasantly.

"Indeed." Cyrus reached into his jacket pocket and extracted a folded piece of paper. "A signature will do." He glanced at the robed man. "And that of a witness."

"Davis," Charles said to the butler. "Take the ladies into the parlour." He looked at Theo again. "You can enjoy a glass of something if you wish and then we'll get started."

Theo felt horribly stung and betrayed. A bit of business. Is that what she was? Mildred motioned for her to follow the butler, and so she did. But only because she had no choice. It was beginning to infuriate her. She felt heat rising to her skin. Once they were in the parlour, she and Greta would make a mad dash from the place. They could overpower Mildred. In fact, Theo looked forward to it. They wouldn't have much of a chance to actually get away, but it would be worth the attempt. It would at least show they were not going to lie down and be walked over like a carpet.

She entered the parlour first since the butler motioned them in rather than walk in himself. Little did the lazy man know that that worked in their favor. Her gaze went to the open French doors leading to the back yard. It was a small gasp from Greta that made her look in the other direction to where Dab stood across the room. Her knees went weak, and tears filled her eyes.

"What is this?" Mildred demanded. "What are you doing here?"

Dab came closer to Theo, ignoring Mildred. "Are you alright?" he asked when he reached her.

She had no power of speech.

"You must be Mr. Adams," Greta marveled.

"And you must be Greta," he returned. "It's a great pleasure to meet you."

Mildred pushed in between them. "My husband will be outraged to find you here!"

"I am here as a guest of the master of this house," he returned agreeably. "Your husband has nothing to say about it."

"She," Mildred said jabbing a finger toward Theo, "—is getting married in a few minutes."

Dab looked more amused than anything. "I did hear something to that effect. I cannot claim to believe it but, if I am mistaken, I will have a front row seat, I suppose." He paused. "You were at the Betrothal Ball, were you not? If so, you will know that Theo and I are betrothed. It was announced. It's been written about rather profusely since."

Mildred was livid. "I do not care what shenanigans you managed to—"

"There is some champagne over here," Dab interrupted. "Would you ladies like some?" he asked, directing to Theo and Greta.

Both girls nodded. "Please," Greta added, glancing sideways at Theo worriedly.

"Go get my husband," Mildred shrieked at the butler.

He walked away with an unhurried step. Was that a smirk on his face? What in the world was happening? How was Dab here? Theo had a dozen burning questions and no powers of speech.

"Why don't we sit?" Greta suggested gently, slipping an arm around her.

Cyrus handed over the document he'd had drawn up. It was an acknowledgment that his debt, thirty-one thousand pounds, was hereby paid in full. Charles took it and perused the contents. He looked up with a rueful expression. "I do apologize. I failed to introduce you. Mr. Cyrus Martel, Viscount Chausterfield, this is Magistrate Sir Herbert Smithers."

"A pleasure," Cyrus said dryly.

Sir Herbert grunted.

Charles looked back to the document and then tore it in two, letting them drop to the floor.

Cyrus was aghast. "What in blue blazes!"

Charles looked to Sir Herbert.

"Charges have been leveled against you, Lord Chausterfield," Sir Herbert stated ominously.

Cyrus blanched. "What is this?" he demanded, glaring at Charles Pugh.

Charles pursed his lips before replying. "You know, at first, I thought you were simply a brother desirous of seeing your sister married to a suitable gentleman … or a rich man," he added with a self-deprecating grin and gesture to himself. "Especially one to whom you owed a tidy sum. But now I know you're merely a self-serving man who has never been close to any of his stepsisters. In fact, you've offered nothing but hostility toward them. You threatened Theodora to get her to do your bidding."

Charles was red in the face with anger.

"When she got away from you, you and two hired men forced their way into the residence at fifteen Barton Street and forcibly removed Greta Martel against her will. You brought her to your house where she was kept under lock and key. You used her to get Theodora under your control."

"Fifteen Barton Street belongs to me," Cyrus thundered. "It is mine! I have the right to do anything I want there. Including forcibly remove my stepsister."

"I first thought it was kidnapping," Charles continued conversationally. "But Sir Herbert informed me I was wrong."

"Dead wrong," retorted Cyrus.

Charles nodded. "It turns out that the charge of kidnapping is only for children fourteen and under. Obviously, Greta is beyond that."

Cyrus glowered. "Yes, she is."

Charles looked to the magistrate who had been watching the discourse dispassionately. "Lord Chausterfield," Sir Herbert said. "As a stipendiary magistrate, I tell you it is an offence to abduct any woman with the intention that she should marry. I've also been informed that you imprisoned the ladies in your home. So, while the charge of kidnapping is not applicable, abduction and false imprisonment are."

"We are leaving," Cyrus declared, addressing it to Charles. "You have destroyed your chance to have Theodora."

"Leave," Charles said pleasantly. "I rather think you should. But you will not be taking either of your half-sisters. Not now and not ever."

Cyrus scoffed.

"It seems to me," the magistrate spoke up. "The best course of action all around is for you to take your wife and go home. Forget this business. Leave your sisters to conduct their own lives. I could charge you, however, the publicity would not be in the best interest of the young ladies, and I am quite certain you would prefer to avoid it."

Mildred came rushing out, breathless with indignation and frustration. She opened her mouth to speak, but Cyrus lifted a hand to halt it. "We are leaving," he bit out.

She pointed behind her. "Dabney Adams is here. He is in there with them." She directed a withering look at Charles Pugh.

"We are leaving," Cyrus repeated. "Get to the carriage."

Her jaw dropped.

"Now!" Cyrus thundered.

She jumped from his shock of his outburst and then walked to the door, humiliated and holding herself rigidly. The butler, who had appeared, opened it for her. She did not so much as glance at him as she walked by.

Cyrus turned to follow her.

"Oh, one more thing, Chausterfield," Charles said.

Cyrus turned back.

"Your debt to me is due. I'll give you until Friday at five o'clock to produce it before I level charges."

Cyrus's face was tight, and his fists clenched as he left.

"Not a happy man," Sir Herbert commented when he was gone.

"No, he's not. And after he'd thought it would be such a joyous occasion."

Sir Herbert chuckled.

Charles offered his hand and Sir Herbert shook it. "Thank you, sir."

"You're welcome. It will please Lady Vinson," he added with an impish twinkle in his eye. "And that makes me happy."

"Care to join us for some refreshments?"

"No. You young people go ahead. I've places to go and all that."

When Charles walked into the parlour, the other three stopped talking and looked at him. They stood in a huddle, each with a glass of champagne. "He's gone," he announced.

"Thank you," Theo uttered shakily.

"Yes," Greta seconded. "Thank you. However did you manage it?"

Charles gestured to Dab. "With the help of this man. When I left you all after tea, I walked outside wondering what to do next. I looked over and there was Mr. Adams sitting in his carriage glaring at me. Trying to glare a hole right through me, as a matter of fact."

Dab laughed guiltily. "I knew I couldn't very well burst into the house and get you both out of there, but I had to see the place for myself."

"I recognized him, of course," Charles continued. "So, I walked over and asked if he wanted to have a conversation. He did and so we did. Luckily, he'd already started wheels turning. It was through his friend's aunt that we were able to get the magistrate's help. Sir Herbert made all the difference."

"So we're free?" Greta asked. "Really, truly free?"

"Yes," Charles replied happily. "Free to do as you will. My suggestion is that we celebrate, and when you're ready, I will see you taken to any location you wish to go to."

"I will happily bring you myself," Dab offered.

"We're so grateful," Theo said, directing it to Charles first and then Dab. "It feels as if our lives have been handed back to us." She realized what she'd said and threw a startled look toward Charles with a gasp. "I'm so sorry. I meant no offense."

He grinned. "Nor was any taken. I told you I wanted to be your friend and I meant it. Who you marry is the most important decision one ever makes."

"I'll drink to that," Dab said.

"Then I shall pour myself a glass and join you all," Charles said before starting for the impressively stocked sideboard.

"And tell us every word that was exchanged," Dab said with a smile. "I can hardly wait to hear."

Charles chuckled. "I shall play it out for you and do my best to impress you with my skill as a thespian."

An hour and a half later, Dab drove the phaeton and Theo sat next to him. Greta sat in middle of the backseat, tipsy and feverishly happy. Theo hadn't tippled much champagne. She was too shaken by Dab's presence and all that had happened that afternoon. He had come to her rescue again.

"I have been handed a new life," Greta proclaimed. "I am free of the guilt I carried. We are free of Hib." Greta leaned up, resting her arms on the seat behind them. "Do you really think Mr. Pugh will call on us?"

Theo grinned and turned to her sister. Greta was not only tipsy, she was infatuated with Charles Pugh. And while he had been the perfect gentleman from the moment they'd met, not allowing his gaze to linger too long on her pretty younger sister, Theo sensed the same feeling from him. "I do."

"And you wouldn't mind?"

Theo's grin turned into a full-fledged smile, especially as she noticed the expression on Dab's face. He seemed to be thoroughly enjoying himself. That fact alone made her heart sing. "Of course not. I would be glad of it. I think very highly of him."

"So do I," Greta said wistfully, as if it was not clear to see. She sighed dreamily and leaned back in the seat again.

"We are not used to champagne," Theo said to Dab.

"I could get used to it," Greta rejoined.

The girls decided that they would go to Cissy's house after stopping at Bert and Mary's to let them know what had transpired. The delight the older couple felt to see Theo and Dab and to meet Greta was heartwarming. The Turners agreed the girls should see their sisters, but they invited them both to return. Rooms would be prepared for them. Theo would have hers and Greta the one next to it.

"Thank you so much," Theo replied. "But we still have the house and Maeve. She needs to know what happened."

"Are you not worried Hib will bully his way in again?" Mary fretted.

Dab nodded. He was concerned about it. Chausterfield would want vengeance if nothing else.

"It's nearly dinner time," Mary added. "Stay for it and perhaps for the night."

Theo glanced at Greta, who was agreeable to anything, and then looked at Dab.

"We could send word to Cissy and Laurel," he suggested. "Let them know you're both safe and out of his clutches. I'll return for you tomorrow and take you to your sister's ... or to see Maeve first. Either way I'll let Maeve know what's happened tonight."

She nodded. "Thank you," she said to Mary. She glanced at Bert who was always amenable. "Do you feel like you've inherited two more daughters?"

"Yes," Mary said boldly. "And I would take two or three more."

"My Mary could have handled a dozen children," Bert said. "And been thrilled with it."

She leaned against him, nudging his arm playfully. "You, as well, my dear."

He chuckled in agreement.

Between the excitement of the day, the sleepless night that preceded it, and the champagne, Greta was tired enough to drop in her tracks. As Theo wrote notes to her elder sisters, Mary took Greta up to get settled in. Theo finished the notes and gave them to Dab before walking him to the door.

He turned back to face her. "I'll be back ... shall we say late morning?" he asked. "Ten o'clock?"

"That would be perfect."

They stood a foot apart facing one another. It was time for him to go but he was reluctant to leave her. He stepped closer and kissed her cheek. A loose curl tickled his nose, but her warmth and scent stirred his blood. Her skin was so soft.

She gave him a tender smile before sobering. "How can I begin to thank you?"

"There's nothing to thank me for. I met you and...everything changed. I didn't *rescue* you for your sake alone. It was for mine."

"I've wondered," she said just above a whisper. "If you feel even a fraction of what I do." Tears gleamed in her eyes.

He took hold of her hands, shaking his head slowly. "If this feeling that so fills my heart that my chest feels tight, as if it's being crushed at times, if this was a fraction of what anyone felt, they would surely be dead. It would not be survivable."

She sighed softly and a tear escaped her grasp before she smiled joyously.

"I haven't stopped thinking about you since I first laid eyes on you," he admitted. "I was captured by you that first moment. When you hid behind me on the veranda, I would have done anything to protect you."

She nodded. "I wanted to say there. It was the safest I'd felt in so long."

As she gazed into his eyes, there was such love there that he felt bathed in its warm glow. Her glow. Maeve had been right. She was the light. But was it too soon to say the words? Was it too soon when he felt them? He hadn't believed he was capable of this feeling, of falling in love. Now he knew. Not only was he capable of it, he was there. It was her. "I love you."

"I love you, too," she returned.

Now that he'd said the words, he wanted to keep saying them. Over and over again. How strangely freeing they were! He loved her with every fiber of his being. He wanted to shout it. He held back because a man, especially an Englishman, kept control of his emotions. At least, how he displayed those emotions. "You're trembling," he said.

"Yes, I am," she laughed. "I believe you might be, as well."

It was true. "I am not a rich man, Theo. I will always protect you, I swear it, but we will not know wealth. I have a title and a house but little else. There is a summer cottage and some land in Hertfordshire, but the house has been shut up for years."

"Do you think I care about any of that? I love *you*. I would not care if you were a pauper. If you were in debt. I want a life with you, too, and I promise you that is enough. We will make our way. And we will be so happy."

He pulled her close, enveloping her in his arms as he kissed her. They held one another crushingly tight, and the kiss went deeper. It was a claiming kiss on both their parts, and it was the best thing he'd ever felt.

By the time Dab had seen Maeve, and sent Theo's notes on to Cissy and Laurel, it was midnight when he returned home. A light burned in the office, and he found his mother there, pacing the floor. "Hello," he said.

She turned to him. "How did it go?"

"It was beyond perfect."

"Oh, darling. I'm so glad."

He took a few steps in. "I'm going to marry her, Mother. I love her."

She smiled. "I know you do. And I think she is wonderful. I've heard it said that mothers are never pleased with the wives their sons take, but Theo is wonderful. I believe the two of you will be very happy."

"I think so, too. I thought you might tell me how outrageous it was when we haven't known one another long."

"No."

He smiled in gratitude. "Were you waiting up for me?"

"I've been wondering what happened," she admitted. "But I'm also having one of those nights when I can't settle into anything." She paused. "I've been thinking a change of scenery might be a good thing for me."

"Oh?"

"Unless you'd rather I not, I'm going to go stay with my sister for a month or two."

"I want you to do what you need to do. How long has it been since you've seen her?"

"She visited a year ago. It was a nice visit." She sighed. "How things can change in a year."

Or a month, or a single hour. "Yes."

"I miss him," she said brokenly.

He walked over and embraced her. Her clutch was tight.

"It's left such a hole in me," she said, needing to express it. "An endless void. Sometimes it feels unendurable."

He didn't speak for a moment. "That will ease with time," he said softly. "That's what the wise men tell us."

She nodded and pulled back. "I know." She dried her eyes.

He gave her a tender smile. "Tell me again how you met."

She nearly laughed. "You know the story."

"I'd still like to hear you tell it. It's been a long time."

Her smiled turned wistful. "It was a beautiful day in May at the church social. I was eighteen."

He did know the story. His father had been twenty-two, and she had first seen him as part of what should have been the winning

143

team in a three-legged race. Until the dapper and athletic Henry Adams had caught his first glimpse of her and tripped, literally falling head over heels. Yes, Dab knew the story, but the light in her eyes was worth everything.

Chapter Eighteen

*W*hen Theo answered the door the next morning, she looked glorious. "Good morning," she greeted, exuding joy.

"Good morning yourself," Dab returned. "You look happy."

She pulled him in and lifted on her toes to kiss his lips before the door was even shut. "I am."

"And now I am," he said.

"My sisters were here this morning," she said. "They've gone to see Maeve, and Greta went with them. I thought you and I could go together and I'll prepare you on the way."

He laughed. "Prepare me?" He couldn't wipe the smile from his face because this was what it would be like to be married to the most wonderful woman in the world. He was so fortunate, so unbelievably fortunate, and he would endeavor every day of his life to deserve her.

"Maeve shared that your parents had an amazing love story," Dab said as he drove toward Barton Street.

"They did. Not the usual one, if there is such a thing. My father was thirty-six when he met my mother. Like you, he had a title and a house, the Barton Street house, but not a great deal of money." She paused. "Papa loved the sea, and he had a fascination with ships so, through one circumstance after another, he wound up in Dover working with a shipbuilder."

Circumstances and destiny, perhaps.

"By that time, he'd lost his first wife. Cyrus was nine. My mother was only nineteen at the time."

"Ah."

She nodded. "You can imagine what people thought, old lecher and young beauty. But it wasn't like that. My parents were the best of friends and silly in love. They were our role models."

A misty drizzle had begun but the rain seemed to hang in the air more than fall. The hood was in place in case it grew heavier.

"All my life, I wondered if it takes a certain temperament for the sort of love my parents had," she mused. "I thought at first that Cissy settled for her husband Hamish. That he came along, and she thought … this is good enough. I thought the same thing when Laurel married Ben. But now I realize that just because there isn't an obvious, splendid romance, doesn't mean the love isn't real. My sisters have strong, happy marriages with good men."

He nodded. "So far, my friends have had splendid romances for the most part. Nigel and Alice did, although it was fraught with drama."

"Oh?"

He nodded. "And Joel and Jane. Do you know they merely passed one another, in a cemetery of all places, and their connection was made. Then when they saw each other next, again just a chance encounter at a ball, it was a done thing. Of course, then they were kept apart because of various circumstances that both of them suffered for. So there was drama there, too."

She grinned. "We've had our fair share of drama, I'd say."

He nodded. It would make a marvelous story for their children one day. "Tell me about Cissy."

"She is responsible and maternal. She looks like my father. She and Hamish have two children, Noel, he's almost eight, and Scarlett, named after my mother. She's five. Laurel and Ben have three little girls, so you can imagine the chaos at family gatherings."

"It sounds fun."

She looked at him hopefully. "Does it really?"

"Yes," he said emphatically. He was so ready for the joyful chaos.

"I'm glad you think so. I've always loved having a lot of family around. Your mother said they wanted more children."

He glanced at her, surprised. "Did she?"

She nodded.

"I would have liked having a sibling." They rode in silence for awhile with the rain tapping on the hood. "Who does Laurel look like?"

"I'd say she's an equal mix of my mother and father. She's more forthright than the rest of us. She doesn't much believe in keeping her opinions to herself. We have been known to complain about it from time to time, but she maintains that her opinions are like well wishes, most effective when shared with those that deserve it."

He laughed.

"I look more like Mamma than my elder sisters, but Greta looks the most like her."

It was quiet for a few moments before he asked, "And Rose?"

She smiled. "She looked like Papa. She'd been a *big* surprise, but that just made her all the more wonderful. She looked like Papa, but she was a mama's girl. Shy and sweet. She used to say the funniest things. She loved peppermint drops and the color yellow." Theo looked away to collect her emotions.

"Does it help to talk about it?" He asked it tenderly.

"Yes," she replied, turning to him. "Now, it does. I want you to know who they were. Mamma and Papa and Rose. They're such a big part of me."

"I want to. I want to know everything that's important to you. I want to be a part of it as much as I can." As the rain grew steadier, he pulled over under the canopy of a large oak and turned to her. "How soon can we be married?"

She blinked. "How soon can it be arranged?"

"Soon." He kissed her. "Not soon enough for me, but soon."

Chapter Nineteen

George Adams had offered a meeting time of four o'clock. His doorbell rang at seven minutes after the hour. He pursed his lips and twiddled his thumbs for a few minutes and then opened the front door to admit his guest. *Guest.* It wasn't quite the right description.

Florence Adams was clearly astonished to see him standing there.

They stared at one another for long moments until he spoke. "You look good, Florrie. You've hardly aged."

She lifted her chin a notch. "I cannot say the same for you."

"And I cannot argue against the obvious." He stepped back and gestured her inside. "But I'm confident we'll find something else to argue about."

She stepped inside, holding herself stiffly. "Where is White?"

"Drinking himself silly if he has any sense. It's the staff's week off." He closed the door. "We do it every year. The few weeks we used to spend in Bath? They always had one of those weeks off. Don't you remember? Or perhaps you didn't realize it. You never were one to pay much attention to anyone other than yourself."

She scowled at the admonition but did not remark on it.

"Shall we have a drink as we discuss whatever there is to discuss?" he asked.

"Why all the sudden?" she challenged suspiciously.

He gave her a puzzled look. "You've asked for this meeting often enough."

"And been ignored or insulted."

"Leave if you want," he said evenly. "Don't behave as if being here is doing me some sort of favor. What are you always harping on about? Arrangements need to be made. A settlement between us." He paused and shrugged. "I've come to agree. I want to be done with the old, ugly chapters of my life."

Her eyes narrowed at the word ugly. "So do I."

"Hopefully that is what we will do, then. Care for a glass of wine or something stronger perhaps? I know I do." He turned and walked on without waiting for her response. In the drawing room, he headed for the sideboard.

"I'll pour my own," she snapped.

He stopped and turned back to her. "Help yourself." He went back to his seat and picked up his half-full glass of claret while admiring her figure. She had kept remarkably fit. Her face was unlined, her auburn hair without a trace of gray. Perhaps sinful living resulted in longevity.

She selected a wine glass and sauntered back to the table beside him to pour from the nearly empty decanter next to him. She emptied the last of it into her glass and smiled tightly.

"Surely, you saw that I opened a bottle of good Bordeaux for you," he said. "It used to be your favorite."

"I saw it, but this will do."

He smirked. "What? Afraid I poisoned it?"

She shrugged. "Perhaps."

"Do you think I want to be done with the wretched chapters of our past only to start a new one by going to prison for poisoning you?" He shook his head. "Not tempting."

She sat across from him primly and sipped. "How do we begin?"

"Why don't we state our objectives? You tell me what you want. I'll tell you what I want."

She bristled with resentment. "I want a fair settlement."

He sipped and studied her. "What is it you would consider a fair settlement?"

"I want a house of my own and fifty thousand pounds."

"And I would like to soar like a seagull," he returned glibly.

"You banished me from this house and from decent society! You have no idea what it was like to have to return home as a grown woman with nothing and no place to go."

"I banished you from this house with good reason, but I made no attempt whatsoever to have you banished from society."

She huffed a bitter laugh. "You are not an idiot. One led to the other. You know that very well."

"I am not an idiot," he agreed pleasantly. "I did quite well for myself, all in all."

She glared. "Oh, yes. The company thrives."

"It does. Although I sold it."

Her jaw dropped and her eyes bulged. "What? When?"

"A few years ago. An offer came my way, and I'd satisfied my business ambition. Achieved all I wanted or needed. So … why not, I thought?"

Clearly, she was thrown by the revelation. She sipped her wine to buy a moment. "I see."

He held back a satisfied smile knowing that she'd probably had his net worth investigated based on the current success of the business. "You needn't worry," he finally said. "I made out well enough to give you the settlement you deserve."

She studied him, trying to decipher his tone.

"You didn't ask what I wanted from this meeting," he mused.

"What is it you want, George?"

"Very simply, the truth."

"What truth? What are you talking about?"

"I think you know."

"I certainly do not."

"I want the truth about the boys you seduced. How many were there? Why did you do it?"

She shook her head. "I will not sit here and get insulted like this. You stumbled upon a few occasions that you misunderstood. I was not even given a chance to explain."

He sighed. There would be no truth from her. She wasn't capable of it. Had he really expected it? What would it have mattered anyway? Those *occurrences* had done the damage they had. He had wanted the truth, though. Wanted to understand her motivation, even if it was madness, even if it was a compulsion she could not stop. "You explained the first time. At least the first time I know about. With my young nephew, although it was all lies."

"What sort of settlement can you live with?" she asked impatiently. "What is it you have in mind? If we are not going to discuss that, I am finished with this interrogation."

"I have justice in mind, Florence," he replied tiredly. "For both of us." He finished his glass of wine and rose. He fetched the Bordeaux, poured himself a glass and hoisted it up before taking a drink. "See? Not poisoned." He sat again and set the bottle aside. "Delicious, in fact."

"I want this over with today! Our marriage is over."

"I agree on both counts."

"I have no wish to stay in the city, by the way. Once I leave this house, you will never see me again. I want to start over somewhere new. Bath or Brighton. A small house will do. Just be fair!"

"You want to live by the sea then."

"Yes, I do."

"You always did enjoy the seaside." He paused. "I saw Charlotte and Dabney a few days ago." She flinched slightly. "He's fully grown, a fine man. So handsome."

"I read the papers" she snapped.

"It made me wonder what a child of ours would have been like."

She looked down at her glass. "Some things were not meant to be."

"Have you looked into acquiring a home in Brighton or Bath?"

"A bit."

"And?"

"Brighton is more expensive."

"That's hardly a surprise. It's become very popular."

"Naturally, everything depends on the settlement," she stated. She gave a small cough and touched her throat. She took another sip.

"My guess is that you have your heart set on Brighton, and you have found the perfect house." He paused. He could see by her reaction it was true. "I understand the appeal. A fashionable seaside resort only some fifty miles from the city. Rather the best of both worlds. Tell me about it."

"The house?"

"Yes."

She cleared her throat and took a drink. "Are you serious about this or are you toying with me?"

His expression grew earnest. "I have never been more serious. I want it over between us once and for all."

She'd finished her wine, so he rose again and offered the bottle. She accepted the pour. Sitting back down again, he said, "You should know that I am going to leave my estate to Dabney. I want him to have it all."

She flushed and narrowed her eyes at him.

"Other than what you get," he added. "But I will not have you coming back for more."

"I suppose you will have me sign off on that. Some sort of contract you've already drawn up?"

"Yes. Correct." He set his glass aside, got back up and went to the mahogany cabinet where he retrieved a packet of banknotes and a bulky bundle of silk. It was an old shawl of hers. He carried the things back to her as she watched with wide eyes. He offered her the shawl first.

She took it, surprised by the weight and feel of it. She set it on her lap and opened it to find a lady's pistol with extra balls and a capped vial of gun powder. She looked up at him with an incredulous expression.

"It's part of your settlement. To be used for protection … or revenge if you so wish," he explained. "Do you know how to load it?"

She looked vaguely insulted. "Of course, I know how to load it."

"And this is the rest of your settlement," he said handing over the packet. "What you are truly interested in. In order to leave with that, you will need to sign a document that releases me from further payment to you."

She looked inside the packet and coughed lightly. "How much is it?"

He returned to his seat before replying. "Twenty thousand pounds. I think a generous amount, given the circumstances."

She was livid. "What circumstances? This is outrageous. You've made millions. I know you have. This is a pittance!"

"There will not be more, Florence. The *circumstances* are that you seduced and molested boys. I could divorce you for adultery. I would have done it except that it would have shamed me as well as you. It would have shamed my family. Dab. If the truth came out."

"I never molested anyone! I never forced anyone to do anything." She coughed again and frowned with discomfort.

"Are you alright? Are you ill?"

"No! You have distressed me. Talking of molestation."

"Perhaps it's well-deserved shame and remorse choking you."

"No, it is not," she bit out through clenched teeth.

"No, I know it's not." He paused. "It's the prussic acid in the wine."

She blanched. "What?"

"I believe you heard me. Prussic acid. Hydrogen cyanide. It was in the last of the wine in the decanter. You consumed a fatal dose. That's why your skin is prickling with heat and your heart is pumping and your throat is closing. The poison is ravaging your internal organs. You have only minutes or perhaps moments to live."

She shook her head in denial, but she knew it was true. She had felt perfectly well upon her arrival and now she was suffering. "Murderer!"

"Yes. Well, you ruined my life and you harmed innocent boys. I decided your crimes were worthy of death. Call me both judge and executioner."

She gasped for air and clawed at her throat. "They will know," she rasped. "People knew I was coming here. You will be hung!"

He nodded. "People did know you were coming here," he agreed. "I made a point of letting them know. This is exceedingly well planned out, Florrie."

She gaped in disbelief.

"The last thing I did before I sold the company was to make a batch of prussic acid precisely for this meeting. You've been living on borrowed time and did not even know it."

153

She picked up the gun and pointed it at him with shaking hands. "You," she said under her breath.

It was exactly as he'd expected and planned on. He reached for the bottle and poured some of it in the decanter to dispel any poison left behind. Swirling it, he said. "The gun is loaded but choose your target wisely. You can shoot me, of course, it's understandable really, but you'll have to reload before you can shoot yourself. I would advise that, by the way. These last minutes will be agonizing."

Already she couldn't breathe. She glared at him and pulled the trigger.

He dropped the decanter. Her aim was relatively true; she'd hit the center of his chest. It was not an instant kill, but it would be quick enough. He did not care about the pain. He deserved it. He welcomed it. He had planned their end well and he ought to enjoy it as best he could.

She started to rise, but collapsed, unable to draw breath. Shaking hard, she scrambled to reload the gun.

The servants would return tomorrow to a gruesome scene, but he'd made accommodations for them. He'd seen his lawyer only yesterday to review and amend his will. He'd explained at the time that Florence had never stopped hounding him for a settlement and that he planned to see her and offer twenty-thousand pounds and a house somewhere, if need be. He had set the stage.

Now, slumped in his favorite armchair, bleeding profusely, he watched her fumbling with the pistol, desperate to end her agony. He hoped she could manage it because their deaths *had* to appear as a murder suicide with her as the guilty party.

More than once, he had considered suicide. He was ready for his life to be over, but self-murder was a crime punishable by the forfeiture of one's estate. The Crown did not need his estate, his nephew did. It was Dab's recompense.

The pistol fired again and she fell back. She had only managed to shoot herself in the throat, so she was not dead yet, but she would be. Who would die first was the only question, and that was good enough for him. When her befuddled gaze found his, he smiled.

Chapter Twenty

*D*ab and Nigel sat in the office looking over some charts as Nigel explained his basic principles of investing. Dab didn't have much capital to venture but neither had Nigel when he began, and he had more than tripled his money. Nigel's advice was to invest in steel. The shipping industry was thriving and there was strong speculation about a railroad being built.

"If I was a betting man," Nigel said, "—of course, my father cured me of any desire for that, but if I was, I would wager that we'll see it in the next twenty years. I believe railway travel will become commonplace for our children."

Dab smiled at the idea of children.

Nigel grinned. "About that lovestruck smile on your face, how is Theo?"

"Wonderful."

"When will the two of you tie the knot?" Nigel teased.

"Soon." It was amusing to see the grin disappear from Nigel's face.

Nigel leaned back. "You are serious," he said in awe.

"I am. It can't be soon enough for me."

Nigel laughed. "That's fabulous!"

"So far, I'm not getting any lectures about how quickly it's all come about."

"I am looking right at you, my friend. I see the happiness and the assurance in your face. And I know how quickly it can happen."

"I suppose you do. But I swear, Nigel, I did not think I would join the ranks. And I'm just so grateful that—" He broke off as emotion choked his voice.

"I know," Nigel said. "I understand completely. Do the others know?"

"No. It's all come about so quickly. But the wedding will be simple and quiet, a small affair held at the church her elder sisters attend. It will likely just be her family in attendance since my mother is in Bedford, and all of you will be in the country by then. Later, we'll do a reception of some sort with everyone. I really don't care a thing about the wedding, other than to get it done."

Nigel nodded. "I felt the exact same way."

"When are you leaving for Merton Park?"

"The plan is for Thursday."

"Are you still going on to Manoria after that?"

"I hope so. We'd like to. Perhaps in October. It all depends on how Alice is feeling."

There was something about the way Nigel said it. "How she's feeling?" Dab repeated.

Nigel looked smug.

Dab tried to withhold a smile. "Is there something you want to tell me?"

"Something like ... what?" Nigel asked innocently.

"Oh, I don't know. Perhaps something about a new little Walston joining the human race in the coming months?"

Nigel's smile broadened. "We are not announcing it yet. Alice insists on waiting at least another month. Although *she* wasted no time telling her sister and her aunt, and then my sisters. And, of course, she wrote to her family."

Dab chuckled.

"She was gracious enough to allow me to be there when my parents were told."

"They must be over the moon."

Nigel nodded. "They are."

"Their first grandchild. Congratulations. Do you hope for a boy?"

"Either that or a girl. I definitely want one or the other."

Dab laughed and Nigel joined him.

"I don't care which it is," Nigel said.

"I am thrilled for you both. How is Alice feeling?"

Nigel's smile vanished. "Terribly sick in the morning. That part of it is not enjoyable. Hopefully, it won't last much longer. I would have gotten her to the fresh air of the country before now except for that she has been so sick."

"I'm sorry to hear it."

"The doctor reports that it's normal. Some pregnancies are like that. But it's dreadful. Some days, she can't keep much down. And strong smells will absolutely set her to retching."

Dab looked to the door as he heard footsteps approaching.

Fanning appeared. "Excuse me for interrupting," the butler said. "But there is someone here to see you, my lord. He says it's urgent."

"I need to be going, anyway." Nigel stood. "Between her sister and my sisters, she is being waited on hand and foot, but I still don't like to be gone for too long."

Dab rose to his feet and offered his hand, and they shook. "Congratulations again. And thank you for your counsel."

"You're welcome to it. You should consult with your friend Mr. Pugh. He might have good advice. A bit of insider knowledge."

Dab nodded thoughtfully. "I suppose he might."

"If anything looks promising, let me know," Nigel said as he started for the door.

Dab followed. "You know I will. Give my best to Alice. I hope she feels better soon."

"You know who will probably go into mourning over your marriage? The press. No more Adonis to write about."

"I do hope so," Dab said dryly.

The stranger waiting in the foyer held a leather satchel. He was in his fifties, lean and balding. "May I help you?" Dab asked once Nigel had gone.

"You are Dabney Adams?"

"I am."

"Forgive me. I should have said Lord Sonden."

"I will never take offense to being called by my name," Dab replied lightly.

"I'm Dalton Egan. I was your uncle's friend and solicitor for many years."

Dab cocked his head. Why in the world would the man be here?

"Is there somewhere we can talk?"

"Of course. This way." Dab led the way to the parlour where the men sat. "May I offer you some tea or—"

"No, thank you. I'm here on business. Sad business. I'm sorry to be the one to tell you, but your uncle is gone. Dead, I mean to say," he added apologetically.

Dab was taken aback. "I just saw him days ago," Dab stammered. "Not even a week ago.

The man nodded. "He mentioned it."

"I don't understand. How? He didn't look well but … he didn't seem close to death."

"No, he wasn't. The truth is, and it is a shocking truth, he was shot and killed by his estranged wife yesterday."

Dab gasped.

"And then she killed herself in the same manner. Murder, suicide."

Dab was breathless, he was so stunned. Florence. After all this time. Might the altercation have had something to do with him? With what he'd revealed?

"She had pursued him for years about arranging some sort of settlement between them," Egan said.

Dab nodded. His uncle had said as much.

"She wanted to move on with her life, and he did as well. He said he was ready to be done with it."

Dab hadn't gotten the impression George ever wanted to see her again.

"George had arrived at the amount he was prepared to offer, so long as she would leave him in peace. Twenty thousand pounds."

The amount was staggering. George had despised Florence.

"To be perfectly honest," Egan continued. "I thought it was on the low side, given his assets."

Dab blinked. Twenty thousand pounds was on the low side?

"But he merely informed me. He did not ask my opinion. And I feel certain there were mitigating circumstances I was not privy to." He paused. "I will say, he seemed very calm and settled about it all," Egan said pensively. "This was only the day before yesterday."

A shiver came over Dab. "Really," he breathed.

Egan nodded. "He saw me because he wanted to make a few amendments to his will."

Dab experienced another shiver, sharper, straight down his spine.

"He couldn't have expected what happened, but I cannot help but wonder if there wasn't some sort of … intuition involved. Him shoring up his estate right before—" His sentence trailed off.

"It's hard to grasp this," Dab said.

"I know it is. I only learned this morning and felt the exact same. A policeman called on me."

"Exactly what happened? And where?"

"The incident occurred in his home. In the parlour. We can't know exactly what happened because the servants had the day off. But we know that she showed up at the time they'd arranged. Four o'clock. They must have talked and had some wine, and he had offered the settlement. We know that because the packet of money was … there with an agreement I had drawn up stating that, with her acceptance of the funds, he was released from any further remuneration. It was, in essence, a settlement of divorce even though there was no official divorce."

It was so shocking; it was difficult to think clearly, but it did seem well thought out.

"Your uncle's cook arrived back at seven in the evening, only a few hours after it happened. She was the one who found them." Egan paused. "I don't know how many details you want, but there would have been no surviving the wounds. He was shot in the chest. Then she turned the gun on herself hitting here," he said touching his throat. "She had to have planned it or at least thought shooting him was a possibility because she had the gun."

159

Dab shook his head. He would have thought Florence was the last person to ever kill herself. "I thought I would see him again," Dab said.

"I'm sorry that it won't be possible. He held you in high regard. He left his estate to you."

Dab felt himself jerk. "To me?"

"Are you really so surprised?" Egan asked gently. "You are his closest blood relative."

Dab drew breath to explain that he, too, had been estranged from his uncle, but he refrained. If Egan did not know it, he did not need to.

"I am sorry for your loss," Egan said.

Loss did not seem a quite fair description since he had written his uncle off more than a decade ago. Their visit and the fact that George had tried to make amends had changed his feelings, but now George was gone? Dab was bone-chilled and shaken.

"I feel like I lost him years ago," Egan continued. "Whatever happened with his wife devastated him. He withdrew from everyone and everything." Egan opened his satchel and pulled out a file which he handed to Dab. "This is a copy of the will and a breakdown of the assets. I am the executor of the estate, so don't hesitate to call on me with any questions you may have."

Dab nodded numbly. "Thank you."

"On a different matter, your uncle made it clear that he did not want a funeral."

"I see."

He closed his case. "I expect it will be in the newspapers tomorrow, which is why I needed to see you today."

"Thank you for telling me."

Egan nodded. "Of course."

The men stood, Egan offered his hand and Dab shook it before seeing him out. When Dab returned, he sank back into the chair, his mind spinning. His uncle dead. Shot. By Florence. In the parlour where they'd visited only a week ago.

Fanning appeared at the door. "He's gone?"

"Yes."

"I'm sorry. I was—"

"It's fine," Dab said.

"Are you alright, my lord?"

Dab looked at him. "My uncle is dead. My aunt shot him and then shot herself."

Fanning gawked. "What?" He came closer. "Shot? Dead? Both of them?"

Dab nodded. "Mother and I just saw him."

"I know," Fanning replied. "I cannot believe it."

Dab understood the feeling. "He left his estate to me."

"Did he? Well. I'm sorry the poor man is dead, but it's good that the estate will go to you. It should go to you." He huffed in astonishment. "Shot by his wife who then shot herself," he repeated. "Where did this happen?"

"In his house. Yesterday."

Fanning cringed. "I hope they've cleaned up the mess," he said without thinking. A split second later he looked appalled.

It struck Dab as funny, although he held back a laugh until he choked on it.

"Oh, I do apologize," Fanning said. "It just slipped out."

"I know. And it's not … funny," he said still laughing. Neither of them was quite able to control themselves so Fanning walked away trying to look chagrined. It was difficult to manage when gripped by wildly inappropriate humor.

Dab quickly sobered. For weeks, he had been wondering how he would claw his way to financial stability, and he'd just been handed a fortune? It didn't feel real. What was real was the scandal that would soon erupt, one that he would be featured in.

He got up to write to his mother. Then he would go see Theo.

~~~

When the post arrived the following day, Dab had yet another shock in store for him, a letter from his uncle. Dab took it into the office before opening it. He broke the seal, pulled out the elegant cream-coloured parchment and began to read.

161

Dear Dabney,

By now, you will have learned that I am gone from this life. You will have been told that your aunt murdered me and then killed herself. How can I know this when she is not due to arrive here for another three hours?

Rather than provide specifics, just know I am a man who is determined to right old wrongs. I am making these final choices, Dabney, and I am resolute in them. I am so terribly sorry for the part I unwittingly played when you were harmed in this very house. I hope you can forgive me.

I received a kind letter from your mother after our brief visit and it gave me some peace of mind, but I want permanent peace. All that must be done first is to put in motion what I planned years ago. I am so very glad that you are my heir. I want you to enjoy what I leave you what I worked for. That gives me strength and purpose. Wealth does not bring happiness or contentment or a harmony of mind, but you saw the love your parents had for one another. It is possible to find such a love. I wish that for you.

Believe it or not, this is the most contented I have felt in years. I am picturing you happy and fulfilled with a lady who deserves you. I am picturing you with children who bring you great joy. God bless you, nephew.

Your uncle,
George

Dab set down the letter and exhaled heavily.

Chapter Twenty-One

On the twenty-second of September, Dab stood in the front of a small chapel facing the gathering of family and friends as the chime-like music of a lyre floated in the air. The music was lovely and ethereal, but not relaxing. Not to him. He was antsy to see his bride and get married. He wanted it so much, he couldn't help fearing something or someone would swoop in and steal away the possibility before he had a chance to latch onto her with both hands and never let go.

His mother had returned for the wedding with her sister, his Aunt Ida, and his cousins, fifteen-year-old Edwin and seventeen-year-old Penelope. Theo's family filled five rows with her elder sisters and brothers-in-law, nieces and nephew, plus the aunts, uncles, and cousins who made the journey from Dover. He'd met them all in the last few days, and they accepted him with open arms.

Rather than travel to Merton Park with Nigel and Alice, as they'd planned, Lakely and Jonathan had stayed behind to be here. Hugh was in attendance, as was Lady Vinson who stood next to her niece. JG and Jocelyn sat together, and they had moved over to allow Charles Pugh to sit next to them.

The biggest surprise of the morning was that Joel, Jonathan's twin brother, and his wife Jane had shown up for the ceremony. Five-year-old Arthur sat next to his mother. Behind them, Bert and Mary looked proud and happy. For someone who had felt isolated for much of his life, Dab was deeply moved to be surrounded by this atmosphere of love and belonging.

Greta entered the chapel wearing pale pink, with a bundle of flowers in her hand. She reached the front of the church and then Theo followed. Her gown was simple, but lovely. A veil framed her face like a halo. She reached him, handed her bouquet to her sister, and Dab and Theo clutched hands. Were they supposed to do that? He didn't remember and he didn't care. He never wanted to let go of her.

"Dearly beloved," the pastor began. "We are gathered together here in the sight of God, and in the face of this congregation, to join together this man and this woman in holy Matrimony, which is an honorable estate, instituted of God in the time of man's innocence, signifying unto us the mystical union that is betwixt Christ and his church—"

The pastor went on, but the words blurred and lost meaning. Dab could only think of her, his beautiful Theo. If only his father and her parents and baby sister could have been there, it would have been perfect. He would have invited his uncle, too. Perhaps it could have been the beginning of a reconciliation between the brothers. Were they all here in spirit? *Yes.* He believed they were.

"… nor taken in hand, unadvisedly, lightly or wantonly. But reverently, discreetly, advisedly, soberly, and in the fear of God."

How many times had Dab thought the word *perfect* of late? Life would not be perfect. He didn't expect or even want it to be perfect. It would be challenging sometimes. He couldn't wait for the challenges. He and Theo would overcome them all and end up stronger for it. Tears filled his eyes and he had to concentrate to keep them in check. She saw anyway and smiled because the strength of her love matched his.

"Therefore, if any man can show any just cause why they may not lawfully be joined together, let him speak now or else forever hold his peace."

Thank God. It was about over.

"Dabney, wilt thou have this woman to thy wedded wife, to live together after God's ordinance in the holy estate of matrimony? Wilt thou love her, comfort her, honour, and keep her in sickness and in health; and, forsaking all others, keep thee only unto her, so long as ye both shall live?"

"I will," he said without looking away from her.

"Theodora," the pastor said, shifting his gaze to her. "Wilt thou have this man to thy wedded husband, to live together after God's ordinance in the holy estate of matrimony? Wilt thou obey him, and serve him, love, honour, and keep him in sickness and in health; and, forsaking all others, keep thee only unto him, so long as ye both shall live?'

"I will," she answered clearly and strongly.

"Dab," the minister said under his breath.

It was his turn and he was more than ready. "I, Dabney William Adams, take thee, Theodora Elisabeth Anne Martel, to my wedded wife, to have and to hold from this day forward, for better for worse, for richer for poorer, in sickness and in health, to love and to cherish, till death us do part, according to God's holy ordinance; and thereto I plight thee my troth."

"I, Theodora Elisabeth Anne Martel, take thee, Dabney William Henry Adams, to my wedded husband, to have and to hold from this day forward, for better or worse, for richer or poorer, in sickness and in health, to love, cherish, and to obey, till death us do part, according to God's holy ordinance; and thereto I give thee my troth."

Dab let go of her hands to reach into his pocket for the ring. She handed him her left hand and he slid the ring on it, where it would remain for the rest of her life. What a wonderful thought. "With this ring, I thee wed, with my body I thee worship, and with all my worldly goods I thee endow: In the Name of the Father, and of the Son, and of the Holy Ghost. Amen."

Theo reached back for her sister, who transferred a ring. Dab had had it made. He wanted one on his finger, as well. It was a simple band, the interior inscribed with the date. She slid it on his finger and then looked up at him, still holding his left hand in both of hers. "With this ring, I thee wed, with my body I thee worship, and with all my worldly goods I thee endow: In the Name of the Father, and of the Son, and of the Holy Ghost. Amen."

"Let us pray," the minister said. "Oh, Eternal God, Creator and Preserver of all mankind, Giver of all spiritual grace, the Author of everlasting life: Send thy blessing upon these thy servants, this man and this woman, whom we bless in thy Name. May they keep the vow and covenant betwixt them made, whereof these rings given and received is a token and pledge, and may ever remain in perfect love and peace together, and live according to thy laws; through Jesus Christ our Lord. Amen."

Dab felt a light touch on his shoulder, but no one stood behind him. *His father.*

"Those whom God hath joined together let no man put asunder. For as much as Dabney and Theo have consented together in holy wedlock and have witnessed the same before God and this company, I pronounce that they be man and wife together. In the Name of the Father, and of the Son, and of the Holy Ghost. Amen."

A wedding feast was held at the home of Charles Pugh, and Charles had lined up carriages for all who needed them to get there. If he was showing off a bit, it was for good reason, and her name was Greta. Dab fully expected their wedding within a year.

Again, perfect. Just perfect.

Society's Spectaculars

Wedding bells for London's Adonis? Many have scoffed at the notion despite the announcement of his engagement at the Betrothal Ball to one Miss Theodora Martel. It was a mere stunt, some declared. Dabney Adams, Lord Sonden since the demise of his father, could not possibly be engaged. After all, who was she? Where did she come from? Why hadn't they been seen together?

Readers, doubt no longer. What a heartrending nuptial it was! Honor, simplicity and, dare I say, love were on full display. Lord Sonden stood in a small parish church awaiting his bride. He wore a white cravat and a silver and white waistcoat below a dark cut-away tailed jacket, more devastatingly handsome than ever. Who could pair up against him? I felt rather sorry for the bride at that moment, for she would surely pale in comparison.

A truly beautiful bridesmaid entered, the bride's sister, Miss Greta Martel. One could not help but notice that a certain wealthy shipping magnate in the congregation could not tear his eyes from her.

The bride entered.

Like many, I had seen Miss Martel at the Betrothal Ball. She struck many, this author included, as possessing a simple prettiness at best, but it also must be said that most eyes were on Adonis who had never looked quite so sure of himself and his choices. He appeared to be smitten.

Astonishing, really, for a man who had been so publicly impassive.

For her wedding, Theodora Martel wore a simple gown, white lace over satin, with short puff sleeves, and long white gloves. A ring of blossoms on her head was attached to a veil so light it almost floated. She carried a bouquet of orange flowers that left a sweet wake of fragrance.

It must be said that she is not merely pretty, she is lovely, and clearly as enamored with her new husband as he is with her. It is real and it is done. Adonis has wed Venus.

Chapter Twenty-Two

*I*n the pale light of morning, Theo shifted and started to get out of bed. "No," Dab complained, pulling her back. She laughed. "It is morning and I have to go."

He pouted. "Go where?"

"I mean *go*," she said, pulling from him.

"Oh, alright."

She grabbed her robe and left the bedroom for the privy. When she returned, he was sitting on the side of the bed having pulled on his breeches. He gave her a wicked smile. "How do married people get anything done?"

"Out of necessity. You do realize we've been abed for much of the week."

He stood and stretched. "I know, but as soon as I'm doing something else, I want to climb back in with you."

She came closer and kissed him. "Me, too."

He ran his hands up and down her back. "I like that about you," he murmured as he admired the view down her robe. "Do you still want to go today?"

"To see Standon Cottage? Of course, I do. I can't wait to see it."

"It will be ramshackle," he warned.

"It will be an adventure, and I adore adventures. Besides, I am prepared for however ramshackle it is."

"So be it, my lady. We'll have breakfast and go."

They drove toward Hertfordshire in a sleek, new phaeton. The vehicle had newly designed springs, so it was comfortable even on rougher roads. It was pulled by two horses, so it could cover twenty-five miles an hour.

169

In the last few weeks, Dab had paid off all the household bills and purchased the carriage and two horses, well-matched Cleveland Bays that stood sixteen hands high. The servants had received a raise in their salaries, and a housekeeper and boot boy had been hired.

Dab had also purchased the Barton Street townhome anonymously at considerably below its value, so Greta could continue living there tucked beneath Maeve's safe wing. Apparently, Chausterfield was desperate for funds since all his creditors had called in his debts. It was rumored Sir Amos had been behind that bit of vengeance.

For Dab, the strangest thing about suddenly having abundant funds at his disposal was that nothing felt terribly different. The fortune didn't feel certain and permanent. What if it was discovered that George was the mastermind behind his own death and that of his wife's? It had, in fact, been a double crime. Dab refused to worry over the matter, though. That would negate the gift of the inheritance.

Instead, he went about placing funds in various places, some of them untouchable and anonymous. He invested. He made purchases wisely and paid for each thing in full. Each one was a thrill and felt like a gift from his uncle. No matter what occurred in the future, he and Theo would handle it together.

Hertford was larger and more impressive than Dab remembered with a surprising number of mansions and parks. Landed gentry, successful bankers, politicians, and wealthy Londoners had built homes here. A mansion called Hertford House took up an entire side of a large garden square.

Dab and Theo stopped at The Golden Maple, an elegant inn, for tea and sandwiches and to reserve a room for the night before continuing onto the cottage. Dab was tempted to simply go to their room and stay the rest of the day, but Theo was anxious to see the cottage. Or so she said until they were shown to the spacious room, and he took her in his arms and kissed her.

In the grand scheme of things, what did a delay of a few hours matter?

The late afternoon drive toward the cottage was pleasant, despite the rutted road.

"It's here, somewhere," Dab said as they searched for the driveway to the cottage. The woods along the road were dense, the leaves beginning to don an autumnal splendor. "We couldn't have missed it."

"Is it there?" Theo asked, pointing ahead to a break in the trees. "I don't know."

They reached it, but it was so covered in weeds and the encroachment of underbrush, it was hard to make out that it had been a driveway. As they started down it, one thing was clear. No one had tended to it for some time. "Who is the caretaker?" she asked.

"His name is Cross. Frederick Cross. Although caretaker might be a stretch, wouldn't you say? I can't see that any care has been taken. When do you think someone last came this way?"

"Not any time recently," she replied.

And then the driveway opened to a clearing with a house that was larger than she'd expected. The trees, grass and undergrowth had grown wild. A tree had fallen onto the house, damaging the wood-shingled roof.

Dab stopped the carriage and they sat there staring. The stone exterior of the home was multicolored, beiges, browns and pinks, and ivy had covered much of it. The wooden front door was imposing. "The stone is beautiful," she remarked.

"It came from the ruins of an abbey."

"The house has an almost … storybook quality about it," she said.

The comment drew a smile from him.

"Won't it be fun to watch it come back to life?" she asked.

"Yes, it will. Under our direction." He set the brake and climbed down and then helped her down. Even before they reached the front door, they could see it stood slightly ajar. "So glad I brought the keys," he muttered. "I wonder if there's any furniture left." He stepped up and pushed the doors open, allowing the crack of light to widen in invitation.

She followed him inside a great room with cloth-draped furniture. The house seemed far too large to be considered a cottage. She'd imagined a quaint, one-level home with a thatch roof.

"You can see most of the first floor standing here," he said. "What you can't see is the kitchen in that corner, and the staircase, a bathing room and privy on that side."

She looked at the large stone fireplaces and imagined fires blazing in them. One would be nice right now given the chill in the stale air. A dining room sat beyond the great room. Behind it, were lovely windows and an arched back door. She felt certain they had opened to a garden at one time. And would again. Dab was uncovering furniture to inspect it, so she walked into the dining area and pulled the cloth from the table. It was a sturdy wooden table with six chairs, perfect for the home.

She continued into the kitchen with its flagged-stone floor and a hearth and oven on the inside wall. There was a tall, wood worktable in the center of the room. Above it, was a rack with a few hanging pots and pans. She suspected that most had been carted off.

"It's smaller than I remembered," Dab said from the doorway.

"You were smaller," she replied. "It's far larger than I expected."

"Really?"

She nodded. "I love it. I love the rustic charm."

"Ready to see upstairs?"

"Absolutely."

On the upper level, most of the doors stood open. There were two large suites on one side and four smaller bedrooms on another, plus a storage room. They peeked in at covered furniture and some empty spaces with covers left behind.

"Well," he said, standing in the doorway of a small bedchamber. "I guess it was to be expected. I'm going to walk around outside."

Theo, just in front of him, stiffened and grabbed his arm, to stop him. She had not seen as much as sensed someone or something in the room. A definite presence. She sensed fear and alarm and maybe pain. She stepped further in looking around. "Hello?"

"What—" Dab started to ask.

She held up a hand. The presence was a someone. A scared someone. "It's alright," she said soothingly. "We don't mind you being here. Please come out." There was no response, but she spied small feet attached to legs, thin arms wrapped around the legs, and a dark head tucked into her knees. A girl. Pressed against the far side of a wardrobe. "Hello," Theo repeated, squatting down in front of the child.

The girl stayed frozen for several seconds before peeking up at her.

"It's alright," Theo assured her. "Are you alone?"

The girl scowled. She was thin and filthy with stringy, dark hair. "Leave us be!"

Us.

Dab stepped closer to see her and the girl glared at him. "Or I'll kill you," she threatened.

"That's not very nice," he said mildly.

"Go away!"

"The problem with that is … this is our house," he replied.

"You're lying. It ain't nobody's house."

"He is not lying," Theo rejoined. "He hasn't been here for a long time, and I've never been here before, but it is his."

"Ours," Dab corrected.

"If it's his, how come he ain't been here for a long time?"

"We live in London, and he was busy with other things." The girl, who was perhaps seven or eight, was not believing a word they said. "I'm Theo. What is your name?"

"Never heard of no girl named Theo afore," she challenged.

"It's Theodora, but I never liked the name much, so I've always gone by Theo."

"I don't like Theodora either."

Theo had an urge to laugh, but she restrained it. This was a fierce little warrior. "Are you going to tell us your name?"

"No."

"Perhaps we'll make up one for you then," Dab suggested.

The girl narrowed her eyes at him. "I don't care what you do. I ain't gonna answer it." The sound of a muffled sneeze came from under the bed and her expression changed. She jumped up with her fists raised high. "Don't you touch him!"

Theo rose with her as Dab quickly knelt to peer under the bed. He motioned, and out scooted a very young boy, probably four years of age. He stood with his head hung. "What's your name?" Dab asked him gently.

"Boy," the child said quietly.

"Boyd?" Dab repeated.

"Leave him be," the girl shouted.

Theo's heart felt as if it was in a vise. "We're not going to hurt him or you either. How long has it been since you've eaten?"

The girl's fierceness may have dimmed a bit. The boy dashed to the girl who enclosed him in her arms. "We make do. Just leave us alone."

"We can't do that," Dab stated. "As I said, this is our house. Which makes you our responsibility for the time being. It's not that we mind you being here, but we can't simply leave you. We can return you to where you came from or—"

"No! We'll die afore we go back there!"

"Or," Dab said, as if she hadn't interrupted. "We can take you into town with us and get you cleaned up, procure some fresh clothes and a proper meal for you."

She shook her head. "We ain't going back."

Theo sat on the mattress, causing a plume of dust to rise. "I suppose you came from Hertford?"

The girl glowered. "I didn't say so."

"I'll get the food," Dab said.

She nodded and he left. "We brought some food with us, a light picnic, so we'll start with that, shall we?" The small boy peeked around at her, but the girl yanked him back. "Such mean looks you give," Theo said. "We are trying to help you."

"We don't want your help, lady. Bugger off! I ain't stupid. We know this ain't your house."

"It is," Theo retorted. "I do not lie."

"That's a lie right there coz' everyone lies. 'Specially grownups."

"What grownups? The ones at the orphanage?"

"Yeah. That's right. They do. Think you're so smart, don't you? Only I didn't run away from the orphanage. They booted me out a long time ago."

"Booted you out? Do you mean to say you got adopted?"

The girl gave her a withering look. "Don't be daft. Would you adopt me?"

Orphanages did not simply kick young children out. "Not to the workhouse," she reasoned aloud. "You're too young."

The girl scoffed. "You don't know nothing, do you?"

"The orphanage sent you to a workhouse?"

"Mebbe they did and mebbe they didn't. I ain't never going back. I'll die first. You see if I don't."

Theo could not conceive of this waif forced into labor. What work could she be put to? She was relieved to hear Dab returning.

"In my experience, food makes everything better," he said. "Let's spread out the blanket outside and eat a proper picnic. It's too dusty in here."

"Yes," Theo agreed. "That's a good idea." He turned and left, and she looked back to the girl. She was usually good with children, but she hadn't made a bit of progress with this one. Hopefully the thought of filling their stomachs would win out. "We'll go find a good spot for a picnic. Come when you're ready."

"I'm hungry," the boy said to the girl.

Theo bit her bottom lip and held back tears as she walked on. The more she tried forcing the matter, the more the girl would dig in her heels.

Please follow.

The inn had prepared the picnic for them. Fresh bread, chunks of ham, apples, and candied pecans. They'd also sent a bottle of wine and a jug of apple cider. As Dab cleared the ground and spread out a blanket, Theo quietly shared all that had been said.

The children soon followed, the boy eager, the girl suspicious, but both of them quickly tucked into the food. God only knew when and what they had last eaten. "Chew before you swallow," Theo said to the girl, alarmed at how fast she was shoveling it in. At this rate, she would choke. "No one is going to take it away from you."

The girl ignored her.

Dab leaned over on an elbow and gave his wife a look of amusement mixed with pity. "What do children do in the workhouse?" he asked the girl when she finally began to slow down.

"Work," she said with her mouth full.

"You should not speak when your mouth is full," Theo corrected gently.

The girl gave her a sour look. "He asked, didn't he?"

"Work on what?" Dab asked.

The questioning exasperated the girl. "I was sent to the cotton mill with the others. Alright? You happy now? I picked cotton up from under the machines. Grownups are too big and fat to get down there. I'd like to see you get down there."

Dab quirked a brow. "Dare I hope you will speak more civilly when your brain realizes your stomach is full?"

She rolled her eyes.

In the light of day, it seemed clear to Theo that the boy and girl were not full siblings. The girl's hair was straight and dark, and she had a heart shaped face. The boy's build was entirely different. He had kinky lighter hair and green eyes. She selected a bit of ham and nibbled on it wondering what they should do with the children.

The girl peered critically at Dab. "You ever been in a cotton mill, Mister? Cotton's in the air all the time. It floats around and you breathe it in. People cough all the time from it." Her eyes narrowed. "They *die* from it."

He nodded soberly.

"I *hated* the orphanage, and I hated the workhouse, and I hated the mill. And I ain't going back. I'll die afore I do."

"I see," he replied. "Well, how would you feel about going back to the city with us? Londen, I mean to say. After you've been cleaned up and have decent clothes. Tomorrow."

Silence.

"Then what?" She asked as if she had a dozen other offers to consider.

"I don't know, but there's surely a better place for you there than what you've described."

The girl went back to eating, and Dab and Theo exchanged a look.

Nothing was easy over the next few hours. After repeated promises that they would not be taken back to where they came from, the children were transported back to the inn. The girl refused to give her name and she rarely made a civil remark. The children ducked down and hid as they rode through town.

Theo was left to see to their baths and new clothes while Dab sought out the constable before going to find Frederick Cross.

The constable, an overweight man with a flat nose, listened, nodding as if he'd heard the complaint before. "Thing is, sir, Freddy had a stroke four or five years back. He were an invalid after that. He passed on last spring, and it were a blessing, truth to tell. You've been taken in by the brother, Patrick. He's a drunk and a ne'er do well and he were a ne'er do well before he were a drunk. Or maybe they went hand in hand," he said with a shrug.

"I see."

"He will have drunk up your money, sure as I'm sitting here. You can have him locked up for a while for theft maybe, but you'll not get your money back."

"That, at least, explains it," Dab replied. "My parents thought Cross was a good man."

"Frederick were a good man. Patrick is a troublemaking arse who only cares about his next swig of gin. Not to make light of your situation, but you got double crossed."

The pun might have been clever, but Dab was not amused.

"I am sorry for it," the constable added. "Reflects badly on the whole town. Then again, every town has rotten eggs, don't they?"

"They do. I appreciate the information." He started for the door but turned back. "The house needs repairs. Can you recommend someone?"

"Able Sutherby would be your man. He's got two grown sons and a son-in-law to help him. Carpenter, stone mason, you name it, Sutherby and Sons can do it. You'll find him on Mead Lane."

"Thank you, sir." Dab put on his hat and tipped it before leaving.

By the time Dab started back to the inn, he felt confident leaving the repairs in Able Sutherby's hands. He'd also stopped in the orphanage and had a brief but unpleasant encounter with the matron of the facility that led him to believe the place was every bit as harsh and bleak as the girl had indicated.

He had not been permitted to look around. The matron had informed him that if he had a desire to involve himself in the administration of the facility, he should seek a position on its Board of Governors. There had been no kindness or warmth in the woman's manner. Such a person had no business running an orphanage. Where was the oversight and how thorough was it?

He returned to find the children asleep in cots that had been delivered to the room. Theo sat cross-legged on the bed. "They were so tired," she said quietly.

He sat next to her. "How was it?"

She sighed. "Extremely difficult with her. Everything was a struggle. Taking off her clothes. Getting into the tub. Washing her hair. I shouldn't look at her. She didn't need any help."

"They have had a hard road to travel, but we'll see them put on a better one. I think we should take them to Mary and Bert... for advice."

She smiled at the thought. "Yes."

He nodded and grinned.

"By the way," she said. "I did learn her name. They called her Gabby because she had, and I quote, a big, smart mouth."

He shook his head.

"I told her that Gabby was short for Gabrielle, which is a beautiful name. I also told her she could change it if she wanted, but that I liked Gabby." She paused. "She's thinking about it."

"And him?"

"They called him Boy or Nine, because he was the ninth infant brought to the orphanage near about the same time. He hasn't even been given a name. Not that they would say, anyway. I told him he was lucky that he could choose a name for himself. Most people don't get to do that. I suggested several. Actually, I think I suggested every male name that I know."

"I imagine Gabby had opinions on all the suggestions."

"Oh, yes. And he idolizes her. What she says is law."

"Was a decision made?"

"Nathan," she replied with a smile. "Nate."

"I like it. Gabrielle and Nathan."

"Gabby ran away on her way to the mill. Then she went and got Nate out from the orphanage. Snuck him out."

He mulled it over. Her own freedom would have been hard enough to procure, but his had to have been of equal importance to have risked it.

"What did the constable say?" Theo asked.

"He said that Frederick Cross had a stroke and passed on."

"Oh! Oh, dear. But—"

"His brother has been collecting the funds and using them to buy and guzzle gin."

"Oh."

"It's our own fault. The property should have been checked on, and it's not been. The good news is that a man named Abel Sutherby of Sutherby and Sons was recommended for repairs and I met them and feel good about them."

"Then you accomplished quite a bit."

"Not as much as you." He looked over at the children. The girl was curled on her side, her face toward them. "She looks angelic when she sleeps."

Theo looked at her, too. "Yes, but only when she sleeps." She looked back at him. "The wife of the innkeeper helped with the clothing. We owe her for that and for their baths and the cots."

He nodded.

"I worked on getting Gabby to stop saying ain't," she said. "It's not I ain't going back, it's … I will not go back."

"How many more times did she say ain't after you said that?"

Theo donned a thoughtful expression. "A hundred and five, I think. She went out of her way to say it."

He chuckled. "It's not quite the trip we expected, is it?"

She wrapped her hand around his. "No. It's far more remarkable."

Chapter Twenty-Three

ab woke the next morning with Theo curled against
him, her arm draped over his chest. He loved the
feeling of her.

She looked up at him. "We need to find the children's birth
certificates if we can," she said quietly.

"How long have you been awake?"

She grinned. "Not long."

He sat up, glanced at the children, and leaned against the
headboard. "Where shall I look?" he whispered since the children
were still sleeping.

"The orphanage? The workhouse?" She sat alongside him. "If
they are there, we'll probably have to pay something."

"That's fine. I'll gladly do their song and dance."

"Or the parish church perhaps," she mused. "Don't they keep
records of births and deaths?"

He got up and began dressing.

"I don't want it to appear that we're dumping the children off
on Mary and Bert," she added worriedly.

"We're not. We're seeking their advice. I think we both know
how she'll react, and Bert would do anything to please her. But we
are most decidedly not dumping them off. We can keep them, you
know. We both want what's best for them."

She nodded.

He sat again, put on his shoes, and began buttoning his shirt. "Is
she about six, would you say?"

"I think more like seven or eight. She's small, but they are both
undernourished."

Anger roiled within him, taking him by surprise at its ferocity.
He stretched his neck and reached for the cravat he'd worn
yesterday.

She scooted closer and ran a hand over his back to soothe him. "He's probably four," she continued. "They said he was the ninth infant brought in close to the same time, if that helps."

He turned to face her. That seems like a lot of infants brought in about the same time."

She nodded.

"Where are you going?" Gabby asked having hoisted herself up on an elbow.

He looked at her. "I've got some business to take care of," he replied quietly.

She sat straight up with a scowl on her face. "I will not go back," she pledged.

He stood with his hands on his hips. "Oh, for God's sake, Gabby," he said with exasperation. "We're not taking you back. If we were taking you back, why would we not have already done it?"

She pointedly turned away and laid back down, but then turned her face to speak again. "If you're going, hurry up about it. I have to piss and I ain't going to do it with you here."

He huffed in astonishment at the girl's cheek, and then looked back at Theo who was close to apologetic laughter. He leaned down and kissed her. "I'll be back as soon as I can."

Where to start? Dab walked down Peg's Lane toward Shire Hall. If there were a registry office, it would be there. He passed the Hertfordshire Mercury, the newspaper, and stopped short. Newspapers had been a nuisance in his life, but what if one could prove helpful with their abundance of local knowledge? He considered a moment and then went inside.

The distinct smell of paper and ink hit first thing. There were three men busy at work that he could see and a few offices in back. One man was bent over a printing press, his shirt sleeves rolled up. Another toiled at his desk writing something with intense concentration. A man who'd been engaged in setting type looked up at him quizzically. "Help you, sir?"

"May I speak with the editor or a writer?"

The man bobbed his head toward the back. "Young Skerritt is in the first office."

"Thank you." The first office door stood open. Dab knocked lightly on it and a man of perhaps thirty years of age with longish fair hair looked up from copy he was editing and blinked in surprise, presumably to see a stranger lurking in his doorway. "May I help you?"

"I hope so," Dab replied.

"Come in." The man stood and gestured toward a chair. He offered his hand before Dab had reached it. "Paul Skerritt," he said. Skerritt had an intelligent, eager look about him. His nose was sharp and his lips too full for conventional handsomeness, but it was a pleasant visage, just the same.

"Dabney Adams," he said as they shook.

Skerritt drew back. "Are you really?"

"I am."

"Naturally, I get the London papers," he said with a smile. "Sit, please. What brings you this way?"

"Standon Cottage. It's been in my family for generations."

"Lord Sonden," Skerritt murmured with a nod. "I should have put that together. Will you be restoring it … with your new wife?" he added playfully.

Dab grinned. "Yes."

"Congratulations on your marriage."

"Thank you."

Skerritt leaned back, enjoying himself. "So, Dabney Adams. Lord Sonden. Adonis. Will I sound ridiculous if I admit to being delighted to meet you?"

"If you can assist me, I am delighted to meet you," Dab returned lightly.

"I will certainly try. With what may I assist?"

"When my wife and I went to see the cottage yesterday … for the first time in many years—"

"There's a story right there," Skerritt interrupted hopefully.

"Yes, but not the one I'm here about."

"Which is?"

"We found two children inside."

The editor's good-humored expression vanished. "Children?"

Dab nodded. "A girl perhaps seven years of age and a younger boy. They ran away, her from the workhouse, and him from the orphanage. She took him from there. She lived there before they sent her to the workhouse. The workhouse sent her with others to work in a cotton mill."

Skerritt nodded. "Not an easy life and it couldn't have been an easy feat slipping away, either. And then she sneaked into the orphanage and got the boy out?"

"Yes. She is the kind of child who makes up her mind she's going to do something, and then she does it. Anyway, they were half-starved and filthy. We've fed and cleaned them up and we'll be taking them to the city with us to find a new home for them. She is adamant that she will not go back to where she came from."

Skerritt grunted and nodded. "I can't blame her there. The workhouse is a disgrace. It's attached to old Bridewell in Back Street, a gaol for debtors and criminals. I can't say I know much about the orphanage. I assume you mean Founders Children's Home on Fore Street?"

"Yes. I need assistance locating the children's birth records. We are prepared to pay for them. Whatever needs doing. The orphanage seems the most logical place, but the lady I spoke to yesterday was utterly uncooperative."

"Was she? Why don't you and I start there and see if we can't have more success this morning?"

"I appreciate that. Someone local might make all the difference."

"Especially a local who can write a nasty story on the institution if its warranted," he said. He stood and led the way from his office. "We'll arm ourselves with some information first." He stopped at the desk of the man who was still diligently writing. The man looked up.

"Silas, what can you tell us about Founders Children's Home?"

"What do you want to know?"

"Who runs it. Both the person in charge of daily operations and the board of governors."

"And anything else you can tell us," Dab added.

Paul Skerritt gave Dab a look. "I probably should have warned you, we call Silas En*silas*odedia for good reason."

Silas looked smug as he reached for a wooden box full of notecards and began to look through them.

"Dabney Adams, meet Silas Brocket."

Silas looked up at Dab appraisingly. "Pleased to meet you, Mr. Adams, also known as Lord Sonden. Are you here to see about selling your property?"

"See what I mean?" Skerritt asked.

"No," Dabney answered Silas. "We'll be restoring it and spending time here."

Silas swiveled to face the men with a card in his hand. "Glad to hear it. I hate to see a fine house go to rack and ruin. You'll be more than welcome."

"Thank you."

"I remember when the orphanage was begun. I was a lad of nine or ten. A series of tragic events made the necessity of it apparent. The one I recall most clearly, although I didn't bear witness myself, was a pair of infants left on the doorstep of the Congregational church. Newborn babes they were, twins, each swaddled tightly. They must have been left at first light, but it was February."

Dab felt a chill up his back.

"They'd been laid on a coarse blanket with blood on it, evidently the mother's blood, in a sort of cross formation, one babe on bottom with the head of the other placed on its stomach. The one on top had been dead longer. I believe it was a boy and he was blue and stiff. Perhaps it had been a stillborn, we can't really know that, but the other babe was also beyond saving." He paused. "Can you imagine opening the vestibule doors to find that?"

Unfortunately, Dab could and did imagine it.

"Some of the wealthy folk in town became the founders." He glanced at the card. "The orphanage opened its doors in sixty-two. Within a matter of a month, it had sixteen children ranging from infants to six years of age. I suppose older children went to the workhouse. The numbers have grown, of course. There's a report made every year of the number of boys and girls in residence and their ages. I'd say there's at least thirty or forty now. Maybe more."

"Where do they come from?" Dab pondered.

"The orphans?" Silas asked. "Some from the poorest of the poor in Butcherly Green and other places. Folks who can't afford to feed themselves, much less another mouth. Some are there because of a parent or parents who've died or are too sick to care for them." He paused. "Sometimes newborns come from the great houses," he added with a wry expression. "I should say from the servants of great houses, who have found themselves in unfortunate circumstances."

"Sometimes caused by the masters of the great houses," Skerritt said.

"They come from a lot of places," Silas said. "For a lot of reasons."

"Who runs the Home?" Skerritt asked.

Silas consulted the card. "Mrs. A.R. Mitchell was hired as headmistress in August of thirteen. Eight years ago now."

"And the board of governors?" Skerritt asked.

"Let's see. There are five listed, but that includes old Mr. Downing, who died last year. The others are Preston Rountree—"

"Politician," Skerritt said to Dab. "Former MP."

"Miss Delphinia Knight," Silas read.

"The mayor's sister," Skerritt explained. "Involved in several charities."

"Finch and Purkiss."

Skerritt nodded. "Big money, important men." He nodded. "Alright. Thank you, Silas. Shall we?" he said to Dab, gesturing onward.

"Thank you for the information," Dab said to Silas, who nodded.

"They called you young Skerritt," Dab commented as they walked to the Home.

"My father was editor before me. I'll be young Skerritt until I'm gray and bent with age, I imagine."

It wasn't a far walk and they chatted amiably on the way, but both sobered by the time they entered through the front door. The Home was an oppressive place. It was as if the feel of gravity thickened with tension the moment one stepped inside, or was it Dab's imagination?

The office beyond the entrance hall was empty, but both men turned as they heard footsteps approaching. It was the lady he had spoken with the day before. She recognized him, as well, and she did not seem pleased to see him again.

"Mrs. Mitchell," Skerritt said in a friendly enough manner.

She stopped a few feet away from them, her posture very erect, her frown fixed in place. "Yes?" She was a tall woman with wide shoulders and a full bosom. Her hair was dark, her eyebrows thin and arched.

"I'm Paul Skerritt, editor of the Mercury," he introduced. "And this is Lord Sonden. I believe you spoke with him yesterday." She flicked her gaze to Dab momentarily. "May we have a few minutes of your time?"

She complied with a regal nod before continuing into the office. The men exchanged a look and followed, Skerritt taking the lead. She'd gone around her desk, but had not taken a seat, nor did she invite them to sit. "What is it?" she asked.

"May we sit?" Skerritt asked pleasantly. "This may take a few minutes." He sat before she could respond, so Dab did the same. She resentfully took her own seat, her unnatural brows arched even higher. Had she purposely formed them that way? "You've been headmistress for eight years, I believe," Skerritt began.

"That is correct."

"We have several questions about the general running of the place, but in the interest of expediency, as Lord and Lady Sonden are returning to London today, he also has a specific need to see the records on two of your former children. So, we should begin with that."

She cocked her head. "Records?"

187

Dab nodded. "Whatever information you have on their births. Names, parents' names, dates, that sort of thing."

"That is not public information," she snapped.

"No?" Skerritt asked. "Why is that? I feel certain there are not many who ask, but we are asking."

"This is a privately run—"

"It's a charity," Skerritt interjected.

She folded her arms. "The children entrusted to our care—"

The men waited. "Yes?" Skerritt urged.

She flushed with embarrassment. "What possible reason would he have for asking?"

Skerritt looked at Dab.

"My wife and I found two children," he began.

"Found them? Where? Who are you talking about?"

"There was a girl about seven years of age. Gabby, I believe you called her?"

She scowled with disdain. "She is not one of ours any longer. She belongs to the workhouse."

"Belongs to it?" Skerritt repeated. His pleasant expression had vanished. She'd offended him.

"She is a ward there is what I meant to say."

"But she was here," Dab stated. "What can you tell me about her?"

"I can tell you she's the devil's spawn."

Both men waited without a word, although Dab was biting his tongue.

"You have not said why you wish to know," she challenged.

"The children were frightened, dirty and malnourished," Dab stated. "We are taking them to be cared for in a fitting manner. They should have any information about themselves that is available."

She lifted her chin. "The other child is also from the workhouse, I assume?"

"You assume incorrectly, madam. The other child is a boy who came from here. You called him boy or Nine."

"Nine?" Skerritt blurted.

Dab nodded. "He was the ninth infant brought here around the same time. He is four years of age or so."

"What you say is ridiculous," she retorted. "We do not call children by numbers. You say you found him but how do I know you did not take the child?"

"You know who he's referring to then?" Skerritt said.

"A boy did go missing several days ago. William. We called him William. He's a simpleton. Sometimes the only way to get his attention was to shout, 'Boy' at him. Therein lies the confusion, I imagine. Where did you find him?"

"They were in hiding," Dab replied savagely. "You will please provide any and all information about … William," he said sarcastically, "and Gabby."

"And afterwards," Skerritt said, "I would like to see this place. Tour it. Speak to the staff and the children. I would like to see the level of care given here." He paused, glaring right back at her. "Or shall I seek a seat on the board of governors first, Mrs. Mitchell? I believe that is what you said to Lord Sonden yesterday."

"I do not know who this man is," she snapped. "I have a sacred duty, and he marched in here demanding—"

"Basically, he s nobility from London who owns an estate nearby. An estate where he found the children in hiding. He's famous in the city and I imagine he will be here, as well. I wouldn't want him as an enemy."

She might have paled a bit.

"The children's information," Skerritt repeated. "If you please, headmistress."

She rose stiffly and went to a shelf for a ledger. She sat again before going through it. She had not looked at either man since she rose. It took three or four minutes to find it. "Girl child," she read. "Left the third of June, eighteen fourteen, umbilical cord still attached. No identification left with her."

She looked up at Dab.

"When was she sent to the workhouse?" he asked as levelly as he could.

"Two years ago."

"And the boy?"

189

She flipped the page and studied the entries. She flipped another. "He was left in a crate on the fourteenth of October, three years ago. He had his milk teeth."

"There's no other information?"

"No."

"You say he had his milk teeth. What does that mean? He was six months old? A year old?"

She shrugged with indifference. "A year."

"But no name? If he was already a year old, he must have had a name."

"There was no other information provided," she repeated.

"Where did the name William come from?"

"We have to call them something, don't we?"

Skerritt sighed and looked at him. "It's not all you hoped for, I'm sure."

It wasn't, but there was nothing to be done about it. "You don't think there's any other birth records somewhere?"

Skerritt shook his head. "Churches keep baptismal records, but I doubt these children were baptized. So, no. I'm sorry."

Dab stood and offered his hand to Skerritt, who stood to shake it. "Thank you for your help," Dab said. "I'd best be on my way."

"I'll see you again," Skerritt returned.

"Yes." Dab glanced at the headmistress and then started from the room.

"About that tour," Skerritt said to the lady.

Dab smiled and kept going. He was gratified that Paul Skerritt had been unleashed on the place.

Chapter Twenty-Four

Gabby remained taciturn until Hertford was miles behind them. As her mistrust faded, her questions began. What was London like? Did they have children? What did their house look like? Did they eat meat at every meal? The answers led to more questions and opinions and chatter, but it was a nice change.

How many dresses did Theo own? Did they have a maid? Did they have a dog? "I'd like to have a dog," Gabby announced.

"I want a dog," Nate seconded.

"That's only because I said I wanted one," she said to him.

"That's not necessarily true," Theo rejoined. She'd swiveled toward them and her arm rested over the seat.

"Then what kind of a dog do you want?" Gabby challenged him.

"A little one," he said without hesitation.

"That's not a *kind* of dog," she stated.

"You mean the breed?" Theo asked. "Do you have a particular breed in mind?"

Gabby frowned and looked away.

"We had sheepdogs," Theo said. "When I was younger," she added. "Big, fuzzy, wonderful sheepdogs. I miss them."

"Where are they?" Gabby asked.

"One died, but one is still alive. Her name is Jolly. She lives with my cousins now. They have their own dogs that Jolly plays with."

Dab looked at her and she smiled at him and reached over to touch his arm in reassurance. She hadn't mentioned the dogs before.

"Jolly," Nate said with a smile.

"Jolly good, mate," Gabby said in a silly voice, making him laugh.

Dab glanced back at Gabby. "It's jolly good to see the real you instead of that ferocious little fighter we encountered."

"That's because I was hungry. And I didn't believe it was your house." She paused. "Hertford disagreed with me," she announced imperiously.

Theo pressed the backs of her fingers to her mouth to keep from laughing. "It disagreed with you," she repeated when she could control the urge.

"You never had something disagree with you? Like it didn't set right with you."

"I've had something I ate disagree with me," Theo replied.

"Did you get the runs?"

Again, it was hard not to laugh, especially in light of the children's amusement. "That is not a polite question," she said instead.

"What? Don't rich people get the runs?"

Theo faced front, laughing as discreetly as she could. Dab was doing the same thing.

"Rich people don't get the ruuuuuns," Gabby said.

Nate laughed. "Rich people don't get the runs," he repeated.

Theo turned back around to them. "I have a question."

"Is it about the ruuuuuuns?"

Nate kept laughing.

"No. What were some of the other children's names at the orphanage?"

Gabby's smile faded. "Martha, Wanda, Mol, George, Johnny C., John S., Lizzie, Freddy Four. There's lots of them. Why do you want to know?"

"Was there a William?"

"There was a Willem. He works at the paper mill now. There was a Will, but he ran away after he got flogged."

Theo looked at Nate. "Did they ever call you William?"

He frowned and shook his head.

"No," Gabby answered. "Why?"

"I was just curious."

"They called him Nine. Or Boy. Mostly Boy. One of the matrons, Miss Ruth, she didn't like him."

Nate's frown darkened.

"She used to box his ears. Call him stupid. Dumb as a mud fence."

"Well, that's just nonsense," Theo exclaimed. "What a terrible woman."

Gabby nodded. "She boxed everyone's ears, then said it was coz we looked sideways at her, but really she just liked doing it. I'd like to box her ears."

"So would I," Dab muttered.

The children heard it and it made them smile, but Theo shook her head. "She sounds cruel. That sort of thing is very wrong, but you wouldn't want to repeat it."

"Yes, I would," Gabby retorted.

Dab looked at Theo, silently concurring with Gabby. "We know your birthdays," he said over his shoulder.

Gabby frowned. "How do you know that?"

"I went to the Home and asked for the information they had on you. I spoke to Mrs. Mitchell."

"I hate her," Gabby declared.

Theo sighed because of the darkness in her expression and the heat of her words.

"I'm not overly fond of her, myself," Dab said. "Do you want to know your birthdays?"

Gabby scooted forward on the seat. "I do."

"Your birthday is June third. You were born in 1814, which makes you seven. You'll be eight on your next birthday."

"What about Nate?"

"The sixth day of October. He will be five next Saturday."

Gabby looked at Nate with astonishment. "It's almost your birthday!"

Nate was beaming.

"You will be five," Theo repeated with a smile.

"Now," Dab said. "The first thing we're going to do when we get back to the city is go see some friends of ours."

"What friends?" Gabby asked

"Their names are Bert and Mary Turner," Theo replied. "They are very special friends. Dab and I both met them on the night we met."

"Will Nate get a birthday party and a present?" Gabby asked.

Talk about a change of subject. "Yes," Theo replied.

"Will I, when it's my birthday?"

"Yes."

"Do I get to pick out my present?"

"We'll see. I was about to tell you about Mary and Bert."

"Can it be a toy?" Gabby persisted.

Theo glanced at Dab, who was chuckling. "Yes," Theo replied.

"Alright. You can tell us about Mary and Bert. Do they ever get the runs?"

Nate chortled. Dab laughed and shook his head. Theo rolled her eyes, but it was impossible not to be tickled. "Oh, Gabby."

When they reached the Turner's, Gabby surveyed the home. "This is nice. What's this street called?"

"Denbigh," Dab replied.

Gabby had asked about dozens of streets and buildings and landmarks.

They all climbed from the carriage. "Let's walk around back to see the garden," Theo said to the children. "Stretch our legs a bit."

They'd decided that Dab would speak with Mary and Bert, if they were home, to explain the situation and ask any and all advice since the older couple was experienced with children. Theo took hold of Nate's hand, and she and the children walked down the street and around to the backyard garden. "I've worked out here a bit," Theo said. "I like the garden."

"I like it, too," Nate said.

"It's alright," Gabby said with a shrug.

The girl's reticence had crept back. "These are dahlias," Theo said. "What flowers do you like best?"

Nate meandered on to choose his favorite, pondering over each bloom.

"I like the brick walls," Gabby said. "It feels safe. Like you could hide in here."

The words were heart wrenching. "Did you ever play hide and go seek?" Theo asked.

"I played hide," Gabby muttered. "I played pick up the cotton."

How quickly and completely Gabby had gone surly again.

"I like these ones," Nate called.

"That's lavender," Theo said. "Don't they smell lovely? You can put them in a sachet under your pillow at night to help you relax and sleep. You can also make ice cream from it."

Nate looked puzzled. "Ice cream?"

"Have you tasted ice cream?"

He shook his head.

"Oh, lots of times," Gabby said. "With our steak dinners and candy."

"You will like ice cream," she said to Nate, ignoring Gabby's sarcasm.

Gabby bent to smell a flower. "Can I pick one?"

"Yes."

"What's this one?"

"I don't know its proper name. We always called them windflowers."

Gabby picked a pink one. "I know those are roses," Gabby said, pointing in the other direction. "Everyone knows that."

Theo heard Mary rushing out and turned to her with a smile.

"Hello," Mary exclaimed. Tears brimmed in her eyes.

"Hello," Theo returned.

"Oh, you beauty," Mary said to Gabby, who had dropped her flower and stood with a guilty expression. Mary went closer and squatted to be eye to eye with the girl. She reached up and stroked a strand of Gabby's dark hair. "Would you believe my hair used to be this color?"

Theo worried about Gabby's reaction. She nearly gasped when Mary grabbed and hugged the girl. Mary released her and Gabby stood very still, watching warily as Mary looked to Nate and held her hand out in invitation. He came to her at once.

"He looks a bit like Bert," Mary marveled, pulling him into an embrace.

Mary released him and looked back at Gabby. "I am going to need some help getting back up and then what do you say we go see the house together?"

Gabby reached out to help her, and Theo quickly went to her other side.

"These old knees of mine," Mary complained but still with a smile on her face. "I know better than to squat down as if I was a frog."

"A frog," Nate laughed.

Mary sighed wistfully as she looked at the children. "They are just beautiful," she said with a shake of her head.

A tiny smile broke through on Gabby's lips.

Nate was not attempting to hold back his. "I'm Nate!"

"I know you are."

"I'm almost five."

"Practically a young man," Mary said. She looked at Gabby. "And you will be eight in June, I understand."

"June third," Gabby said as if she'd known it all her life.

Theo felt on the verge of tears, and she did not want to cry. "They have never had ice cream, so we must have it for their birthday," she said.

"Of course, we must!" Mary pulled Gabby against her bulk. "What's your favorite color, Gabby?"

"I don't know," Gabby replied quietly.

"The reason I am asking is that I have a perfectly nice room for you, but we may want to make changes once we discover your favorite colors."

Gabby cocked her head. "Are we going to stay here?"

Theo's throat had such a painful lump in it. "Mary," she managed to say under her breath.

"I hope you will," Mary replied to Gabby. She turned to Theo. "Yes, love?"

Theo bit on the inside of her lip. How could she express it in front of the children? She wouldn't hurt their feelings for the world, but Mary had to know they were not simply dropping them on the doorstep. "We ... don't want—"

"Oh, I know, dearest. You don't want to give them up. I understand." She looked at the children with a loving smile before looking back to Theo and giving her a wink. "But you know how we've wanted another boy and girl. They feel like a gift from God. No one will take better care of them than we will."

Theo pressed her lips together and bowed her head. Fat tears escaped her grasp.

Mary went to her at once and pulled her into a strong embrace. "God put you and Dabney in our paths for a reason. You've given us more family to love and enjoy. Yourselves and your sisters and their families and now the children." She pulled back to allow Theo to dry her face. "You and Dab are just beginning married life. And how it agrees with you. You're more beautiful than ever."

Theo fumbled for a handkerchief. "Not at this moment I'm not."

"Yes, you are." She turned back to the children. "My husband, your new papa, is not home at the moment. What a surprise he will have when he gets here! Shall we go in and see the house?"

Nate nodded happily. Gabby nodded more reluctantly.

"Come on!"

Nate ran to her, clasped hold of her hand and they started for the house.

Gabby looked at Theo. "You thought she'd want us?"

"I knew she would. She had a little girl once who died. Mary has had a hole in her heart ever since. She and Bert have a grown son, but he isn't here very often."

Gabby considered for a few moments and then she grinned. "I like her."

Theo smiled, too. "You will love her. I do."

"Will we still see you?"

Theo's smile vanished. "Yes! Of course, you will. We'll all be family now."

"Really?"

Theo made an X over her heart. "Cross my heart."

Gabby looked at the house. "Can we go see it?"

Theo nodded and they started off, but Gabby ran back for the flower she'd picked. "I think I might like pink best," she said as she caught up again. "But maybe blue. Or purple, like lavender. Do you think I could make a sachet? What is a sachet?"

Theo's heart brimmed with excitement and gratitude. She answered Gabby's questions as she led the way inside. As she pointed out the various rooms to Gabby, she noticed the girl's arms were pressed to her chest, her hands clenched together. When they reached the staircase, Theo gestured for her to go ahead. "The bedrooms are upstairs."

They climbed the steps listening to Mary and Nate talking. They followed the voices and found them in a bedroom for children. Theo had only glanced into the room before; she'd been so distracted with the goings-on of her own life. Now she saw it with a new appreciation. There were two beds with colorful, patchwork quilts, two small desks and chairs and a bookshelf with books and toys. The windows in the room looked out over the backyard. The walls had been bright blue, but the paint had faded with time.

Gabby looked around in awe, but, understandably, it was the toys that fascinated her. Nate had dropped to the floor to play with toy soldiers. Gabby looked up at Theo, as if asking for permission, and Theo nodded encouragement. Gabby stepped in, drawn to a china doll. She reached out tentatively and touched its face and then gently lifted a china hand and let it drop. She looked at Mary. "It was your little girl's?"

Mary nodded. "It was. And now it's yours."

Gabby looked at the doll again. "What was her name?"

"My daughter? Or the doll?"

Gabby looked at her. "Your daughter."

Mary smiled. "Amelia."

"That's a pretty name."

Mary nodded. "She was a sweet, happy, wonderful girl. And now I believe she is a sweet, happy angel, waiting for me in heaven."

Gabby looked around at the other toys, but it was the doll that most intrigued her. "What's the doll's name?"

Mary smiled. "Part of the fun of having a doll is getting to name her. You can choose any name you like."

"What did Amelia call her?"

Mary took a moment to reply. "Maisie," Mary managed. "Amelia called her Maisie."

"That's what I was going to name her, too!"

"How wonderful. Then she won't get confused, will she?"

Gabby shook her head and picked the doll up carefully. "I won't break her," she pledged.

Theo turned to step out to the hallway for a moment to collect herself, but Dab stood in the doorway, looking at her with such love and understanding, the tears came anyway. She didn't want to cry in front of anyone and her throat ached from the restraint. As she stepped past him, he handed her his handkerchief and kissed the top of her head. In the hall she held a fist to her mouth to contain a sob.

"This looks fun," Dab said cheerfully as he went into the room.

Oh, dear God. How she loved him. One day, her heart was going to burst from it.

"Introduce me," he said.

"These are soldiers," Nate said.

"Do you know their ranks?"

"What's that?" Nate asked.

The happy chatter continued. When Theo was sufficiently collected, she stepped over to the doorway. Dab sat on the floor with the children while Mary perched on the side of the bed to watch them all. Theo realized she would never forget that image for as long as she lived.

"Are you alright?" Dab asked as they drove home that evening. They'd stayed to dinner and then to tuck in the children.

"Tired," she admitted. "I didn't sleep well last night and—"

"It's been an emotional day," he finished for her. They rode in silence for a few minutes before he added, "But we'll see them next week. And most weeks."

"I know," she said softly.

"Whoa," he called, halting the horses. No one was behind them, so he turned to her. "Are you alright?" he asked again.

"I'm just overwhelm—" she couldn't even finish the word before she blubbered.

He pulled her close and held her. "I know," he said softly.

"I'm sorry."

"Don't you dare be sorry." He kissed her head.

She pulled back and glanced behind them, wiping her face. "You can drive on. I'm fine."

"I love you," he said.

She smiled and sighed. "I love you."

"Get up," he called to the horses, and they started in motion again.

Chapter Twenty-Five

*D*aylight was waning as Theo emerged from the dressmaker's shop. The temperature had dropped sharply since she'd been with the modiste. A brisk late-October wind suddenly gusted, and she bent her head against it as she hurried on. One of the shop's assistants followed close behind with a large box which went in the boot of the carriage.

"Thank you," Theo said.

"You're welcome, Lady Sonden. I hope we'll see you again soon."

Theo hurriedly climbed in the driver's seat and pulled out when the way was clear. She'd driven the cabriolet. She was getting comfortable enough with it that she could enjoy it, although there was more traffic now with people hurrying home to beat the rain she smelled in the air.

She'd enjoyed her afternoon, but it still felt strange to have the financial wherewithal to do as she pleased and to be treated so deferentially. She had been in such a peculiar state of mind the last few days. She was not exactly fretful, but she felt a certain guardedness.

She had never been as happy, and neither had Dab, but she'd begun worrying that it might somehow dissipate or, worse yet, disappear altogether. She'd experienced tragedy. She knew how lives could be changed in an instant. She could not help wondering if it might be better to hold back a small part of herself. Rein in some of her happiness. Protect a piece of her heart in the event of future catastrophe.

The wagon in front of her stopped, so she did likewise. As she waited, the wind gusted, and a few colourful leaves fluttered in the air. There were no trees along New Bond Street, so the sight gave her an unexpected lift.

A decorative crimson flag of a shoppe caught her eye as it flapped in the wind. Two young women dashed by, laughing and shrieking as they tried to catch ribbons that had blown from their shopping bags. One of the girls caught and held a scarlet ribbon that whirled in the wind. Theo smiled at the various flashes of red.

Are you trying to tell me something, Mamma?

She had arrived back at home before she noticed the perfect red leaf that had come to rest on her lap. Yes, her mother, Scarlette Josephine Martel, the beautiful, elegant Lady Chausterfield, was indeed trying to convey something, and Theo knew exactly what it was.

She felt a rush of release. As of this moment, she would stop her senseless fretting. She would not hold back one iota of the love, joy or sheer amazement she felt with her husband and her life, because it was a gift beyond price that should be and would be appreciated every single day.

Dab hurried from the house to unharness the horse and park the carriage for her. He'd gone to Hertford to check on the progress of the cottage that day.

"You're back," she said. "Good. I'm so glad you beat the rain."

"Yes. Me, too. I just arrived." He helped her down but kept his hands around her waist. "Any problems?"

"Of course not," she said with a tap of her gloved hand to his chest. "I'm a thoroughly capable driver."

"Well, you had a thoroughly capable teacher."

She chuckled. "How was everything?"

"Well in hand. They cleared the driveway and cut down the felled tree and repaired the roof. I met all the Sutherby's and the son in law. I like them and I respect their work ethic. Oh, and I saw Paul Skerritt. There is some interesting news there."

"What news?"

"I'll tell you all about it over tea. Let me take care of this first."

"After a kiss, if you please, sir."

He made a face. "Do I have to?"

She pulled him close and kissed him soundly.

"On second thought," he said, "Who cares about the carriage or tea? Let's go to bed."

She laughed and retrieved the box from the boot and started inside, sashaying more than was appropriate for a lady. She looked over her shoulder and found him watching and grinning happily.

A half hour later, Dab and Theo sat on the sofa facing one another as they had tea and hot, buttered toast. A fire blazed in front of them, and a cold rain fell outside. Theo had a warm shawl wrapped around her that was at least ten years old. Dab fingered its frayed edge. "Shall we get you another one of these?"

"It happens to be my favorite. It's the one I wear when I'm sitting with my husband in our own drawing room."

"Fair enough."

"So, you saw Paul Skerritt and … what was interesting?"

"After an investigation of the orphanage, Mrs. Mitchell was sacked. So were three of the staff, including the odious Miss Ruth."

"Good!"

He nodded. "Paul now has a seat on the board. Two of the others resigned, out of shame for the lack of oversight, I suppose. He feels confident with the people who are going to fill the seats."

"That is so wonderful. And to think, none of it would have happened except for finding the children."

He nodded. "I have come to be a big believer in providence these last few months."

She gave him a loving smile.

"Sutherby says the cottage will be finished sometime this spring," he said. "So you have some selections to make, Lady Sonden. Furniture, curtains, carpets, that sort of thing."

The thought was undeniably exciting. "You mean *we* have selections to make, Lord Sonden."

"Yes, I mean we. I always mean we." He paused before asking, "Do I get to see you try on your new gown?"

She puzzled over his phrasing. "Do you want to see the new gown on me, or do you want to see me try it on?"

He gave her a wicked grin and a waggle of his brows.

She laughed and leaned in for a kiss.

Jane Shoup (Super) is the award-winning author of more than twenty novels in several different genres. She lives in Greensboro, North Carolina with her husband Scott, rescue-pup, Gabby, and near her three grown daughters and their families, including six amazing grandchildren.

Visit her website at janeshoup.com